Taking the Ice

by

Jennifer Comeaux

Taking the Ice
by Jennifer Comeaux

Copyright © 2015 Jennifer Comeaux
ISBN 978-0-9904342-3-8
Cover Designed by Sarah Schneider
Photography by Marni Gallagher
Cover Models: Alexandria Shaughnessy and James Morgan

32103589

To all the friends I've made in the skating world
— you make being a fan of this crazy sport so much fun!

TABLE OF CONTENTS

CHAPTER ONE

December, 2013

THE ICY WIND BLEW ACROSS BOSTON COMMON, and I pulled my knit hat down farther over my frozen ears. A large crowd surrounded me, watching the skating exhibition on Frog Pond, but all the body heat in the world couldn't warm the area. It was one of the coldest New Year's Eves I could remember.

My boyfriend Josh moved behind me and sheltered me in his arms, blocking the stinging breeze. I smiled and looked up into his gorgeous blue eyes. Even through the combined six layers we wore, I felt his love and warmth, as I always did whenever he touched me.

"On a scale of one to ten, how happy are you we're not skating in the show this year?" he asked.

I glanced at the shivering girl taking the ice in tights and a thin sweater. "Five hundred."

Since we trained on Cape Cod, Josh and I had performed in the annual show the past two years. But with the national championships only one week after New Year's in the Olympic season, our coaches had instructed us not to skate. We couldn't take any unnecessary risks. Not in the biggest year of our career.

I felt a tap on my puffy jacket, and I turned to see a tiny girl with rosy cheeks staring wide-eyed at Josh and me.

"Hi, Courtney. Can I get a picture with you and Josh?" she asked.

"Sure," we replied in unison and positioned ourselves on either side of the girl. We each stooped and circled our arms around her.

"Thank you so much," her mom said as she snapped the photo.

"No problem," I said. "Will you be at nationals next week?"

The girl nodded vigorously, and her mom hugged her shoulders. "When we heard it was going to be in Boston, we got tickets right away."

"We're pretty stoked, too." Josh grinned and took my hand.

"I'll bet. You're going to have the whole place cheering for you to make the Olympic team."

My stomach churned at the mention of the team, specifically the two spots for pairs. After failing to win a spot twice with my previous partner, my anxiety had been growing stronger every minute the competition neared.

I squeezed Josh's hand to chase away the worry. "I get goose bumps just thinking about it. Everyone we know is coming and bringing ten people with them."

The woman wished us luck, and she and her daughter scooted through the crowd, the little girl watching us the whole way. It hadn't been the first time we'd been asked for a photo that night. As three-time national medalists and the reigning national champions, we'd been featured in a number of Olympic ads. The sponsors had gambled on us being part of the Games by putting our faces on their products. All we had to do was skate awesomely enough to make the team and prove we were worth the gamble. No biggie.

The announcer introduced the next skaters over the crackling sound system, and I cheered while Josh let out a loud whistle.

"Go Caitlin and Ernie!" I yelled for our younger training mates.

They gave us big smiles and charged toward center ice. Since Josh and I were the eldest pair at our rink — at the ripe old ages of twenty-five and twenty-six — all the other teams looked up to us, and we took our roles as leaders seriously. Supporting our friends was the only reason we were standing in the outdoor freezer and not snuggled in front of the TV.

After every lift and throw Caitlin and Ernie completed we cheered vocally as loud as we could since our gloved hands muted our applause. They had a similar look to Josh and me — petite blonde and tall, dark-haired guy — so as they skated I couldn't help but imagine us out there on the ice. When Ernie swung Caitlin up over his head with an easy, fluid motion, my body twitched, knowing the rush of adrenaline Caitlin must have felt. I loved the sensation of flying in the lifts so much.

The music faded away, and Josh and I made sure our friends heard us loud and proud once again. As soon as they left the ice, we made our own exit and hurried under the colorfully-lit trees to the T station at the edge of the Common. We'd parked at my parents' apartment and had taken the train to avoid the crazy holiday traffic.

"Court! Josh!"

We spun around just before we reached the entrance to the station. Our coaches, Emily and Sergei, were striding toward us with their seven-year-old twins. Quinn and Alex's matching blue eyes were barely visible under their scarves and tight hoods.

"I thought you'd left because it was too cold for the kids," I said.

"We didn't want to miss Caitlin and Ernie, so we found a spot blocked from the wind," Sergei said.

A stream of people flowed through the doors, and the six of us fought against the current to get inside. As we descended the stairs, Quinn pulled off her hood and tugged on her scarf, unleashing her golden curls.

"Mom, I'm hot."

"We have to walk to Grandma and Grandpa's when we get off the train, so don't take anything off," Em said.

Sergei looked over at Josh and me as he held on tightly to Alex. "You guys should come to the party for a little while. You know everyone in the family."

I'd lived with Em and Sergei the past six years to save on expenses, so I'd become an honorary member of their family. I could never thank them enough for their generosity.

"I think we're going to head home and watch all the parties on TV," Josh said.

"Yeah, I'm beat. Our slave-driving coaches killed us today." I cast a grin at Em. "I probably won't even make it until midnight."

Josh stopped walking as we landed on the Green line platform. "You have to stay up for midnight."

"Why?"

"Because. It's… it's tradition."

"We both fell asleep at ten-thirty last year." I laughed.

He started to speak and then paused before stumbling again, "But… but next year could be really special. We'll want to remember the moment it started."

I gave him a curious look. We'd been dating four years, and I knew when he wasn't telling me everything. Was he planning a special surprise? My mind went immediately to the one surprise I'd been waiting for… involving a certain important question.

"You don't have to be at the rink until one tomorrow thanks to your *wonderful* coaches." Em poked my arm. "So, have fun tonight and sleep in."

"We're staying up until midnight this year," Alex

announced proudly.

"Well, aren't you two all grown up," I said.

"See, even the kids will be awake. You can't crash early," Josh said.

"Okay, okay." I eyed him again, trying to find a hint of what he was hiding. "You're going to have to entertain me to keep me up."

"I can play every fast-tempo song I know." He smiled and danced his fingers across my shoulder as if it was a piano.

"Ooh, I like that idea."

The D train rumbled into the station, and Josh and I shared hugs and "Happy New Year" wishes with Em, Sergei, and the twins. They continued waiting for the C train to Brookline while we squeezed into the crowded car headed for Chestnut Hill.

I hooked my elbow around one of the metal poles, and Josh gripped it high above my head. The sweet scent of his cologne surrounded me as we pressed together in the cramped space. The train lurched forward, and Josh put his free hand on my waist.

"Do you hear that?" he asked.

I listened over the squealing wheels and heard music from a nearby blaring iPod. The girl behind Josh was wearing earbuds, so I leaned into him to listen closer. The sound of Beyoncé singing "Drunk in Love" came in clearer, and I broke into a grin. Since I'd first downloaded Beyoncé's new album, I'd been obsessed with the song. Josh and I had memorized all the lyrics of the duet, and we lip synched along every time we played it.

"I can't do my moves here." I tickled the exposed skin between his scarf and the back of his beanie. "I'd get thrown off the train for indecent behavior."

Josh's mouth curled into a delicious smile. "We can sing now, but I definitely need a rain check on the moves."

He bent his head close to mine, and we held our own

private, silent concert. Long after the song ended we reached
our stop and were still humming the tune. After a quick visit
with my parents, we hopped into Josh's car and sang out loud
to our favorite CDs all the way to Hyannis Port.

We pulled into the driveway of our friend Mrs. Cassar
and started for the guest house where Josh lived. As we
stepped onto the stone path, the back door of the large main
house opened and Mrs. Cassar called out to us.

"Come inside for a minute, Dears. I have some friends
who want to say hello."

We reversed direction and walked around the heated
pool, and I took off my hat and gloves just inside the kitchen.
Two ladies I recognized from Mrs. Cassar's book club sat at
the table in the breakfast nook.

"Hi, Mrs. Behr, Mrs. Gallagher." I shook their hands, and
Josh followed.

"Take off your coats. Stay a while," Mrs. Behr said.

Josh and I exchanged glances as we shed our jackets. I
knew he was thinking the same thing I was — *Not too long of a
while.*

"Have some champagne. We're toasting early since
midnight is past our bedtime." Mrs. Gallagher reached for the
bottle.

"Oh, they can't have any," Mrs. Cassar said.

The two ladies stared at us for an explanation, and Josh
said, "The only time we drink champagne is after we win a
medal at a competition. It's become our special tradition."

The women let out a collective, "Aww."

"I'm going to buy you a bottle of Dom Pérignon when
you medal at nationals," Mrs. Cassar said.

"You've already bought us so much," I said. "You've paid
for all our skating expenses for four years."

She waved her hand in dismissal. "It's just money. What
else am I going to do with it?"

"Well, if you can't have champagne then have some pie."

Mrs. Gallagher pushed the chocolate dessert forward.

My mouth watered as I could almost taste the silky sweetness. "That looks really good, but we had cannolis in the North End before the show."

"One slice won't hurt," Mrs. Behr said.

"These are elite athletes, Helen. They don't get these hard bodies by stuffing them with sweets." Mrs. Cassar grasped Josh's bicep and then lifted up his sweater and T-shirt. "Look at these abs. You could build a house on them."

Josh's cheeks burned six degrees of pink, and I dissolved into giggles. He pointed his thumb at me.

"She's ripped, too. Wanna see?" He grabbed the hem of my sweater.

I yelped and scooted away from him. "I'm not flashing everyone."

"It's just your stomach, Dear," Mrs. Cassar said. "You walk around here in your bikini in the summer."

"I had to show them mine," Josh said.

I laughed harder. "This party has taken a very sketchy turn."

"You should be proud. I'd kill to be young and not sagging everywhere." Mrs. Cassar touched her wrinkled neck.

Everyone was watching me, so I threw up my hands. "Alright, if you insist."

I gave them just a peek of my stomach, and they whooped and applauded. Josh and I collapsed into more laughter, and I shook my head. Life in Mrs. Cassar's orbit was never dull.

"Are you going to keep skating for fun after you retire from competition?" Mrs. Behr asked. "You can't let those bodies go soft."

"We'd love to do some shows. I'm starting Boston College in the fall, so hopefully I don't put on the freshman fifteen." I patted my stomach. "Josh'll be on the ice a lot more than I will."

"He's become a highly sought-after choreographer," Mrs. Cassar said, sounding like a proud mom.

Josh blushed again, and I kissed his pink cheek. His irresistible shy smile made me want to do a lot more than give him a peck, but the ladies had already gotten enough of a show.

"We should probably get going." I picked up my hat. "We have to rest our wicked abs for training tomorrow."

"Just one more question before you go," Mrs. Behr said. "The two of you are absolutely adorable together. So, when's the wedding?"

Josh and I both froze in the middle of zipping our jackets. I glanced at him, and he just quietly chuckled and kept his head down. Was I supposed to answer?

"They're a little busy with other things right now," Mrs. Cassar said.

I gave her a thank-you smile and a goodnight hug, and Josh and I walked quietly across the backyard to the guest house. Mrs. Behr had no idea how much I'd been asking *myself* her question lately.

Josh hadn't been shy about mentioning marriage until the past few months when he'd gone radio silent on the subject. We'd talked about moving to Boston together in the fall, but no further commitment had been made. Sharing an apartment would be awesome, but I wanted more. I wanted to stand at the altar and look into Josh's eyes and say vows. I wanted to make all our promises official and be his wife. I was ready. But I was starting to wonder if he wasn't.

"Less than two hours until midnight." Josh broke the silence. "What song would you like to hear first?"

He went straight to his high-tech keyboard in the tiny living room, and I sat on the couch, curling my legs under me.

"Umm... how about 'Secrets?'" I said, thinking about my secret wish for a midnight surprise.

"One Republic coming up."

He faced the keyboard, and I angled so I had a direct view of his profile. I had yet to understand how Josh could play so many songs just from memory. It was a mind-boggling talent. He only needed a few moments to collect his thoughts before his fingers began flying over the keys.

Watching him play the piano completely enthralled me every time. He felt the music in his entire body, and the passion came to a head in his strong hands. He poured his soul into the keys in a way that was hotly beautiful.

Time became a non-entity as I lost myself in watching Josh play. When he busted out some ragtime tunes, I got up and danced the Charleston in the narrow space between the sofa and the TV. I didn't realize it was almost midnight until Josh looked at the microwave clock and jerked his hands back from the keyboard.

"Three minutes." He jumped up and went to the bedroom. "I'll be right back."

My heart rate launched into a higher gear, and I dropped onto the sofa. Could Josh be going to get a ring? *The* ring? He'd been so adamant about me staying awake that he had to have a special reason. When he hadn't proposed at Christmas, I'd thought it wasn't happening anytime soon, but he could've been waiting to start the New Year with an extra bang.

Josh returned with one minute to spare, and he held a small, unmarked cardboard box, not a velvet one. My pulse slowed as disappointment sank onto my chest. I wasn't going to say anything to Josh because I didn't want to be *that* girl. The one who harped on getting engaged. Mrs. Cassar had been right anyway. We had so much going on, and I shouldn't be worried about anything past nationals. My heart just hadn't gotten the memo yet…

Josh flipped on the TV, and we counted down along with a million people in Times Square. As the clock hit zero, he pulled me close so the tips of our noses brushed. He set his eyes on mine and spoke onto my lips, "Happy New Year."

We sank into a deep kiss, all softness and heat, and nothing else mattered. Not engagement rings or Olympic rings. With Josh's lips on mine, all I thought of and felt was the overwhelming love he had for me.

We slowly broke apart, and I reconnected with his gaze. "Happy New Year."

He combed his fingers through my long curls. "It's going to be one we always remember."

"Does whatever's in the box have anything to do with that?" I asked.

He smiled. "Partly."

He opened the box and took out a round, red figurine. It had a face on the front and gold designs painted on its sides.

"This is a Daruma from Japan," he said.

I looked closer at the figurine, and one missing feature stood out. "Why doesn't it have eyes?"

"I had the same question. When we were at Grand Prix Final, I was Christmas shopping and saw these, and the first thing I noticed was the blank eyes. I asked the girl in the shop, and she gave me the whole story. At the start of the New Year, you're supposed to set a goal and paint the right eye. The Daruma then serves as a reminder to stay focused on your goal, to keep only positive thoughts. When you reach the goal, you paint the other eye and write what you achieved on the back."

He showed me the empty white heart on the back of the doll, and he pulled two markers from his pocket. "I got blue and green so it can have both our eye colors."

I placed the doll on my palm and ran my thumb over the blank spaces for the eyes. I'd had so much bad juju when it came to making the Olympic team in the past. It couldn't hurt to add whatever good luck symbols we could find.

"What happens if we don't—"

Josh touched his finger to my lips. "Only positive thoughts."

I smiled, and he traced the curve of my mouth. "Which color should we use first?"

"Your choice, my love."

I surveyed them and selected the blue marker. "Do we have to say our goal out loud?"

"I don't think there's an official ritual, but that would be cool."

"Let's hold it together so we can both get the good luck vibes."

We wrapped our hands around the doll, and I started, "Our goal is to skate—"

"At the 2014 Olympics together," Josh echoed me.

We laughed at our unison, perfected from doing countless interviews the past few years.

"Ready to paint?" Josh asked.

I set the tip of the marker to the right eye, and Josh covered my hand with his. We swirled the pen together, painting a solid blue pupil. I capped the marker, and Josh set the doll on his thigh.

"We can bring it to Boston with us," he said.

"And this, too." I picked up the green marker.

Josh beamed at me. "Positive thinking. I love it."

I looked down at the sorta creepy-looking Daruma. The idea of skating at the Olympics with Josh was motivation enough, but now I had an extra motivation to do well in Boston. We *had* to make the team because the last thing I wanted was a one-eyed doll haunting me the rest of my life.

CHAPTER TWO

I TOOK A LONG INHALE OF the cold rink air and exhaled as I stretched my leg atop the boards. Josh and I had checked into the headquarters hotel in the Seaport area of Boston the previous afternoon and were about to begin our first practice. With the main arena still being set up for the event, we were practicing at the Skating Club of Boston, one of the secondary rinks for the week. The small venue should have made me feel at ease, like it was just another training day at home, but the volunteers wearing championship gear reminded me it was no ordinary day. The butterflies in my stomach had already started their wild party.

I switched to doing squats behind the boards, and Josh's black skates walked up beside me. His neon orange blade guards gave him away.

"My mom is here?" he said.

I popped up and followed his eyes to the bleachers. Mrs. Tucker was slowly climbing in her stiletto boots to a spot beside our agent Kristin. She looked down at the bench and wrinkled her nose before wiping it with a tissue. God forbid she get a speck of dirt on her coat. Although, it had probably cost three thousand dollars.

"I can't believe she schlepped all the way out here for practice after getting in so late last night," I said.

"She had to be here in case there are any TV cameras," Josh said.

I let out a dry laugh. Josh's parents had been opposed to our partnership from the beginning because they wanted him to go to law school and join the family practice in Beverly Hills. They also hadn't been fans of our relationship since I wasn't the rich California girl they desired for their son.

All that had magically changed, though, once Josh and I won the national title and were hyped as Olympic hopefuls. Mrs. Tucker had become very interested in inserting herself into our limelight. She was all about us making the Olympic team and giving publicity to her family. Despite her new interest in us, I was pretty sure her feelings toward me hadn't changed. I still felt her contempt whenever she looked at me.

"Poor Kristin," I said. "Your mom's probably giving her an earful about sponsorships she thinks we should have."

"Steph needs to get here and run interference," Josh said.

His sister and I weren't besties, but we'd evolved from enemies into an amicable relationship. Since she was doing a fashion design internship in Los Angeles, she wouldn't be arriving in Boston until the morning of our short program. That left two whole days for Mrs. Tucker to bother us uninterrupted.

The other three teams in our practice group inched closer to the boards, hinting we were moments from the start of the session. On cue, the announcer called all our names, and we left our skate guards with our coaches and took off across the ice.

Josh and I locked hands and sped into identical back crossovers, leaving a stiff breeze in our wake. With all the cool, difficult moves we could do, I still loved doing simple crossovers with Josh the best. We were one entity flying over the ice with just a few powerful strokes, and Josh always kept his eyes on mine, ensuring we were connected in every way.

After we finished warming up, we practiced side-by-side double jumps instead of our standard triples to establish our timing. Usually a double felt loose and easy, but my legs were tight, and having Mrs. Tucker in my sight line didn't help. That woman always unnerved me with her critical stares.

While the program music played for the first team in the group, Josh and I did a few lifts and kept ourselves fresh for our own short program run-through. As the other pair took their bows, we applauded them and then settled into our opening pose. Josh stood behind me, and we faced the smattering of spectators in the bleachers. I could feel Mrs. Tucker's cold glare on me, so I shut my eyes to get into character for the program.

Our flamenco-inspired music began, and Josh slid his hand up my arm, matching the mood of the sensual guitar. We turned to skate eye to eye and moved swiftly across the ice into our first element, the triple twist. I spun quickly in the air and landed neatly in Josh's hands, right on the staccato beat. The twist had always been one of our strongest elements. Any trouble we had usually came on the side-by-side jumps, which were coming up next.

We curved toward the boards, and my legs tightened with nerves again. I pushed off my back inside edge and spun three times, but I was *so* tilted in the air. I came down hard on my hip, and the wet ice soaked my tights. Josh stood tall next to me, having done the triple Salchow cleanly, and I hurried to sync up our strokes.

Josh squeezed my hand, his little sign of encouragement, but I still felt unsteady as we began our intricate footwork sequence. My blades weren't hugging the ice like they should, so I decided to put more oomph into my steps.

And down I went.

That time my butt took the brunt of my fall. Josh kept

going while I scrambled to my feet to resume the straight-line pattern. When we came together at the end of the rink, he squeezed my hand again and said, "Just breathe."

We slowed our pace before the throw triple flip, but I still botched the landing, putting my hand on the ice to balance myself. When we struck our ending pose, I noticed the judges who'd come to watch practice whispering to each other. They were probably saying, "Not exactly Olympic material."

Josh put his arm around my waist, and we skated over to Em and Sergei at the boards. They gave me technical instruction to apply to my Salchow, and I set off to do the jump on my own. I skated around the team doing their run-through and set up for the take-off. Again I was crooked in the air and came down with my arms and legs flailing. My body just wouldn't do what I knew it could. What it had done a million times.

I made two more shaky passes at the jump before Em and Sergei gave me a pep talk and told me to move on to another task. Josh and I did small sections of our long program and wrapped up the session with a two-minute cool down. I toweled the sweat from my face and downed my water as I watched the next group of pairs take the ice. Two of the top challengers for the Olympic team were in the group. I had my eyes trained on them until Mrs. Tucker rose from the bleachers and headed our way.

"We have to get outta here," I told Josh as I stashed my water bottle and shoved my arms in my jacket. "I can't deal with your mom right now."

"I'm right behind you."

We had to cross Mrs. Tucker's path to reach the door, so we race-walked as if we were late. I gave her a little wave and Josh said, "We need to get to the shuttle. We'll catch up with you later."

"You can't talk to your mother for five minutes?" she said.

Oh, gimme a break. She'd barely spoken to Josh for three years and now she was pulling the mother card?

"The bus is leaving in a minute," Josh called over his shoulder. "I'll text you."

During the ride to the hotel I popped in my earbuds and blasted the hardest rock songs on my phone. My goal was to flush the bad practice from my head, but I couldn't stop thinking about how easily my technique had abandoned me.

Once we reached our room, I piddled between the closet and my suitcase for a few minutes before Josh came up behind me and put his hands on my shoulders.

"First practice jitters." He massaged my neck. "That's all it was."

I hung the blouse I was holding and shut the closet door. "When Mark and I competed in our first nationals here, I had a horrible first practice then, too. Also at the Skating Club of Boston."

"And you went on to skate great in the competition. You won a medal."

"I wish we had another practice today. I want to get back out there and prove I can skate the way I know how."

"The best thing to do is let go of what happened today and start new tomorrow. Don't think about trying to prove anything."

I nodded and looked at our Daruma on the nightstand, reminding myself to stay positive, but I couldn't shake the unsettled feeling I had. Josh must have seen the worry on my face.

"I know what you need to clear your mind," he said.

He took his iPod from his bag and plugged it into the speakers we'd brought with us. With a few taps, Beyoncé's sultry voice poured into the room.

"Let it all out." He smiled.

I hesitated, not quite feeling it yet, and Josh shook his head.

"Don't make me do Beyoncé's part," he said, proceeding to lip sync and gyrate his hips Queen B style.

I burst into laughter. "That is so wrong."

"Then you better take the lead." He tapped the iPod. "I'll start the song over."

He turned up the volume, and I felt the bass in my chest. I started off with a subdued performance, but as the song grew in power so did my energy. I tore the rubber band from my ponytail and whipped my hair over my shoulders as I danced my way closer to Josh. The intense way he watched me gave me an added thrill. I leaned into him and rubbed my hands over his T-shirt while silently belting out how drunk in love I was with him.

When Jay-Z began his rap solo, Josh took over, not missing a beat, and I clenched his shirt in my fists. He had to be the least gangsta person on the planet, but he totally pulled off the rap and looked damn sexy doing it.

The song returned to me, and I threw my head back and gave my best lip-synched wail. Josh put his arms around me and crushed our hips together, and we swayed as one for the rest of the song. After the last note, I stood on my toes and pressed a kiss to his lips.

"You were right," I said as I slipped out of his arms. "That was exactly what I needed."

"Where you going?" Josh reached out to me.

I smiled at him and fiddled with the thermostat. "It's kinda hot in here now."

"You want to cool down?"

Before I could turn around, Josh had dropped ice down the back of my tank top. I gasped at the cold burn on my spine and pulled on my shirt to let the cubes fall to the carpet. Josh laughed, and I sized him up.

"You look a little overheated, too." I grabbed a handful of ice from the bucket and tugged on the front of Josh's pants.

"Don't even—" He seized my wrist, but I wriggled free

and held the ice behind my back.

"You gonna give it up?" He grinned and held out his palm.

I narrowed my eyes with determination. "Make me."

He lunged for me, and I shrieked and fell onto the bed. I kept my hands pinned under my back as Josh spread his on the blanket and hovered over me.

"Are you ready to surrender?" he asked.

I shook my head.

He bent his elbows, lowering his long, lean body achingly close to mine. His mouth stayed just out of reach.

"I know all your weak spots," he said, his eyes trailing over me.

My body hummed with anticipation. He angled closer and teased my jaw with feather-light kisses, and I knew exactly where he was headed. He hadn't shaved before practice, and the scrape of his stubble excited my skin. It reminded me of the kisses he gave me in the morning just after waking up.

His lips found my earlobe, and he caught it softly between his teeth. I arched toward him and swallowed the whimper in my throat.

That's one spot.

While his mouth caressed my neck, his hand pushed up my shirt, exposing my stomach. He snaked his fingers over my abs and down to my navel, swirling in a gentle circle. My skin prickled with delight, and the rest of me burned with need. The ice had completely melted in my palm.

I freed my hands and pulled Josh's head to my mouth, slicking his hair with my wet fingers. His tongue dove between my lips, and he groaned as I wrapped one leg around him, pressing our bodies together.

Above the music came a loud rap on the door. I looked in its direction, but Josh nipped on my other earlobe, bringing me back to my happy place.

"Ignore it," he murmured.

The knocking only grew longer and louder, and I couldn't shut it out.

"It might be Em or Sergei," I said, untangling myself from Josh.

He flopped onto his back with a heavy sigh, and I pulled my shirt down and went to answer the door. When I came face to face with Mrs. Tucker, I gave myself a mental kick for not listening to Josh.

"Are you having a party in here?" She marched past me into the room and turned off the iPod. "I don't think you have anything to celebrate after that practice."

I stiffened and balled my hands at my sides. She had *no* right to comment on our skating… on *anything* in our lives. Not after the way she'd treated us for three years.

"I said I'd text you," Josh said.

"I didn't want to wait."

Shocking. Bethany Tucker was the world's expert on being selfish.

"What's so urgent?" Josh asked.

"I'd like to take Courtney shopping for a dress for the Olympic team dinner. There are some excellent boutiques on Newbury Street."

I bit my lip to contain my laughter. I couldn't imagine anything more excruciating than shopping with Josh's mom. In what universe would I want to try on clothes for her and listen to her criticize my appearance?

"Thank you, but I already have a dress," I said. "In case I need it."

"You'd better need it." She shot me a razor-sharp glare, and a cold chill blanketed me.

"Was that all you wanted?" Josh took a step toward the door.

Mrs. Tucker didn't take his hint. "You can't wear a dress you bought at the Cape Cod mall to an event this important.

The photos taken there will be seen around the world."

My face flamed with anger. She was never going to stop belittling me. *Never.*

"It doesn't matter where I got the dress. All that matters is I love it."

I matched her icy stare, and she lifted her pointy chin to peer down at me.

"Well… then I guess I'll see you both at dinner tonight. Kristin is going to join us. There are some new opportunities I want her to explore for you."

"I have plans with my mom," I said.

"Can't you change them?"

"No, I can't. We've been so busy that I haven't seen her much lately. We want to have a quiet dinner before the competition starts."

She not-so-discreetly huffed. "I'll have the concierge make the reservation for three then."

Josh gave me a pained look, and I suspected I'd have to make this up to him in a big way. After his mom finally left, he spread his arms wide.

"Every man for himself?" he said.

"You should've made up something to get out of it."

"You could've told her we had plans together."

"I'm sorry. I was just so happy to have an excuse that it came out before I could think."

He pointed his finger to my breastbone. "You owe me."

"I know." I framed his face with my hands. "You are the best boyfriend and partner ever for taking one for the team."

He pulled me close. "So, how are you planning to make it up to your amazing boyfriend and partner?"

"Hmm…" I spotted the ice bucket and picked up a few cubes. "How about I let you use this any way you'd like?"

I smiled, and he lifted his eyebrows and broke into a devilish grin. Scooping me up with one arm, he carried both me and the bucket to the bed. When we'd melted every last piece, I rolled onto Josh's damp chest and laughed as I almost slid off.

"I've been around ice my whole life, and I can say this with absolute certainty. It has *never* felt that good."

CHAPTER THREE

THE TAXI CRAWLED THROUGH RUSH HOUR traffic on Beacon Street, so I typed a quick text to Mom that I would be a few minutes late for dinner. A few minutes turned into twenty by the time I reached Panificio on Charles Street. I paid the driver and stepped carefully between the mounds of snow piled along the curb.

Inside the cozy bistro, Mom sat at a table near the windows. She gave me a warm smile that matched the feel of the room. I took off my coat, and Mom stood to greet me with a hug.

"Sorry I'm late," I said.

"I should've met you at the hotel restaurant instead of making you fight traffic."

"No, this is perfect. I needed to get away from all the nationals hype for a little while. It gets to be a bit much sometimes, you know? Everyone looking at you, watching who you're talking to, what you're wearing…"

"It's one big show," Mom said.

"And this year is the biggest of all."

The waitress took our drink orders, and I looked around

the dimly-lit room. A candle glowed on each table, but the only other diners were two guys sitting close to the bakery counter. The restaurant was one of my favorite places on Beacon Hill to have dinner with Josh because of its romantic atmosphere.

"Do you remember the first time we came here?" I asked.

"How could I forget? The night after you and Mark won your first national medal."

"I ate a whole pizza." I held my stomach. "And remember how Em and Sergei stayed to have coffee after we left? I wanted to spy on them so bad. I was sure they were going to finally get together that night."

"Took them a little while to get there."

"Not as long as it took me and Josh." I laughed.

The waitress interrupted us, and after we each ordered a pasta dish and handed over our menus, Mom smiled at me over her glass of wine.

"You and Josh are going to have a great story to tell your kids."

"By the time we have kids, we might be too old to remember our story."

She set down her glass and leaned slightly toward me. "You have plenty of time before you need to worry about being old."

"I know, but... I have been thinking a lot about school and my career and marriage and family and... I'm not sure I still want to be a child psychologist. I'm already eight years behind starting college, and I don't think I want to spend that many years in school."

"A PhD is a long road, but it can lead to a very rewarding career."

"So could a teaching degree."

"Teaching?" Mom gave me a surprised look.

I'd been talking about studying child psychology for so long that I wasn't shocked by Mom's reaction. But after I'd postponed college another four years to skate with Josh, I'd taken a hard look at my life plan and realized my priorities had changed. I wanted to establish my career before starting a family, and I didn't want to wait until my mid-thirties to do that.

"Early childhood education," I said. "I love working with kids, especially younger ones, so I think this could be a great alternative."

"Have you researched the education major at BC?"

I nodded and sipped my water. "I can get a master's in five years."

Mom sat back and studied me a few moments. "You know your dad and I just want you to find the right path — the one that leads you to doing something you love. If you think this is something you can be passionate about, then we'll be behind you one hundred percent."

"I've talked to one of the professors and one of the students in the program, and it sounds like it'll be a great fit for me."

"Then you and Josh will both be teachers." Mom smiled. "I'd say you could send him some business, but preschoolers are a little young to learn how to play the piano. Unless they're musical prodigies."

I laughed. "He's super excited to look for studio space in Boston. Some of his students on the Cape love him so much that their parents said they'll drive them all the way up here for lessons."

"That's great he doesn't have to start from scratch in getting students."

"He knows it's going to take time to build up his business, but he'll also be doing choreography on the side, and I'll get a part-time job somewhere. We've been saving a lot too, and this summer we're going to pick up extra shifts at the restaurant since we won't be training anymore."

"You'll be just fine." Mom patted my hand. "Lots of

young married couples are still in school or just starting their careers, and with your skating backgrounds neither of you are strangers to hard work and good time management."

"Young married couple," I repeated as I looked down at the table and fiddled with my silverware. "I hope we'll be one of those."

"Why wouldn't you be?"

I shifted my gaze out the window at the people hurrying down the sidewalk, bundled in their coats. "Josh hasn't mentioned marriage in a long time. I kinda thought we'd be engaged by now."

"Maybe he's waiting to propose at the Olympics."

"Well, that's a little risky," I said and immediately tapped my temples emphatically. "Positive thoughts. I'm supposed to think only positive thoughts."

Mom grasped both my hands and held them warmly in hers. "It sounds like you're thinking about too many things. Just concentrate on doing your best this week."

"This morning was far from my best. But tomorrow... tomorrow I'm going to kill it in practice."

"Dad and I are taking early lunches so we can be there to cheer you on."

"If you see Mrs. Tucker, run in the opposite direction. I swear, I just can't with that woman. If we make—" I stopped and held up one finger. "*When* we make the Olympic team, she'll be on the first plane to Sochi. She's going to somehow get herself on TV every chance she gets. Watch, she'll have her own interview on the TODAY show."

"I wish you were going to have nicer in-laws. You deserve a second family that loves you as their own."

"They don't even love their own as their own." I shook my head. "At least Stephanie and I get along now. She's been great with designing our costumes this year. I mean, I know she did it to get her name out there, but I think she genuinely wants Josh to be happy. I can't say the same for his parents."

"I don't understand people like that. I really don't," Mom said.

"It's good you don't. I'd be worried if you did."

My phone dinged, and I pulled it from my purse to read the text.

Josh: *I'm contemplating stabbing myself with my fork to end this meal.*

I cringed and looked up at Mom. "Josh's dinner isn't going so well."

"Poor guy. I feel for him."

Me: *Do you need more payment from me on my debt to you? :)*

Only a few seconds passed before my phone chimed.

Josh: *Yes, especially since this morning you benefited just as much as I did ;)*

Heat bloomed inside me, and I smiled and returned the phone to my purse.

"Things looking up?" Mom asked.

"Josh helped distract me after my bad practice, so I'm going to help ease his pain after dinner." I lifted my glass to my lips.

"From that smile I think I know how."

My throat spazzed as I swallowed, sending water down my windpipe. I went into a coughing fit that lasted well over a minute.

"You alright?" Mom asked. "I didn't mean to make you choke."

"I'm okay."

I cleared my throat and beat on my chest. Mom and I had gone my entire teen and adult life without any awkward sex conversations. I wanted to keep it that way.

"In all seriousness, I think it's wonderful how you and Josh are always there for each other. You make a great team."

I took a tiny sip of water and swallowed slowly. "We just have to be our greatest for two-and-a-half minutes on Thursday and four minutes on Saturday. Then we'll be able to show the whole world what an amazing team we are."

WITH THE BRIGHT LIGHTS of TD Garden shining overhead, I shaded my eyes and peered into the small crowd scattered throughout the yellow seats. Spotting my parents, I crept closer to the ice door and waved my arms to get their attention. Mom caught my signal and nudged Dad's shoulder. They both waved back and walked through the seats to where I stood in the corner of the rink.

"Hey, Dad." I reached over the railing separating the stands from the tunnel.

He hugged me and then stood tall, straightening his tie. "You hangin' in, Kiddo?"

I smiled and tightened my ponytail. "Be glad you missed yesterday's practice. I promise today will be different."

"Better to work through the nerves now than during the competition."

"That's what I told her last night," Mom said.

A loud boom came from the ice, and I jumped and saw one of my top competitors Roxanne sprawled against the boards. Her partner Evan helped her up, but she shook off his hands and glared at him. I hadn't seen what had caused her fall, but my guess was the quadruple Salchow throw they'd been trying unsuccessfully all season.

"That sounded pretty bad," Mom said.

"I remember when Em and Chris used to practice the quad," I said. "Some of the falls Em took scared me to death."

"I bet she never gave Chris a death stare like that," Dad said.

I laughed. "No, but I wouldn't expect any less from Roxanne."

Evan had won a few national titles with another partner, but Roxanne acted like she was the more accomplished one.

She and Evan had narrowly won the championship over us two years ago, and her obnoxious screams in the kiss and cry had given me extra motivation to beat them the following year.

"Hey, Mr. Carlton." Josh emerged from backstage and shook Dad's hand. He followed with a kiss on Mom's cheek.

"Look, they're trying it again." Dad turned to the ice.

We all watched Evan fling Roxanne into the air. She spun four times but crashed on the landing, earning Evan another scowl.

"I don't know why she's mad at him. She's not checking out for the landing quickly enough," Josh said.

"Because she can do no wrong," I said. "How dare you imply otherwise?"

"I see the rivalry between you is stronger than ever." Dad chuckled.

"Every time Roxanne directs some veiled insult toward us, Em reminds me it's good to have another team pushing us." I tugged harder on my ponytail. "My question is why can't they just let their skating speak for itself?"

"Someone had to take Stephanie's place in getting under your skin." Mom winked.

Josh looked up at the scoreboard. "This session's almost over. We should finish warming up."

My parents returned to their seats, and Josh and I resumed our stretching routine. I replayed all my successfully-executed jumps over and over in my head, not allowing myself to visualize any outcome except perfection.

The announcer gave the teams on the ice a "one minute remaining" notification, and I strode up to the boards, ready to go the moment our session began. When time expired, I ripped off my guards and skated along the boards to the front row where Em and Sergei sat.

"What the hell are Roxanne and Evan doing?" Sergei said.

I looked behind me. They were supposed to have taken their bows and exited with the other teams in their group, but they were just then making their way to center ice.

"That's bush league," Josh said as he took my hand.

We sped away from the boards and pumped our legs in unison, covering more ice with each push. Josh locked his grip around my wrist, and we moved into my favorite warm-up, side-by-side back crossovers. Roxanne and Evan were skating to the ice door, and we zoomed around them with added speed.

Our strokes took us past Em and Sergei, and as we rounded the corner, my right blade caught in the ice. Shock waves of panic bolted through me as I lost both Josh's grip and my footing, and I flew backward. My back slammed into the boards, stealing my breath and stunning me with pain. I bounced off the wooden barrier and slid sideways, slowly coming to a stop. I stayed completely still and tried to catch my breath as my body recovered from the impact.

"Court!" Josh crouched over me. "Did you hit your head?"

I gingerly lifted myself from the ice and winced as I bent my spine. "No, just my back and shoulder."

I'd somehow curled my chin toward my chest so my head wouldn't hit the boards. After Josh's concussion drama a few years ago, my body probably knew instinctively to protect itself from a head injury.

Josh carefully helped me to my feet, and we skated over to Em and Sergei. A burning sensation on my arm briefly took my attention away from the ache in my ribs and shoulder, and I found cuts and scrapes all along my forearm.

"Are you okay?" Sergei asked.

I nodded and picked up my water bottle, but my hand was shaking so badly that I had to set it right back down. The panic and fear I'd felt as I was sliding out of control were now exiting my body in the form of tremors.

Josh put his arm around my waist. "Take as long as you need."

"Let me clean you up," Em said as she dug in her purse.

She brushed my skin with alcohol and put a bandage on the largest cut. Meanwhile, my hand stopped trembling enough for me to sip my water. The fans sitting in the row behind Em and Sergei were watching us and also typing on their phones. Soon the whole world would know I'd wiped out in the first two minutes of our practice.

"Do you want to stay on the session?" Sergei asked. "We can have the doctor check you out now or wait until after."

Pain was still radiating from my shoulder down my back, but it wasn't as strong as before. Moving around and not thinking about it would probably help even more.

"I'm okay to stay."

"If anything doesn't feel right, let us know right away," Em said.

Josh and I rejoined the skater traffic but at a much slower pace. I looked up into the seats where my parents were standing, watching me with concern, and I gave them a thumbs-up sign. Not far from them sat Mrs. Tucker, who held her hand to her head as if she was the one hurting.

We continued our warm-up, but my crossovers were hesitant, not powerful like they usually were. All I could think about was how my Olympic dream had almost ended with a fluke fall. If my head had hit the boards or if my arm had taken the brunt of the impact and had broken, I would be in an ambulance right now. Every step I took on the ice was a potential disaster waiting to happen.

My exterior shaking had ceased, but my insides were still quivering. As we ran through our Muse free skate, I landed every jump and throw on two feet or with a hand on the ice. I didn't trust myself to attack the program. Josh kept encouraging me with "You got this" and "Free and easy," but I couldn't relax.

Sergei ushered me to the medical room backstage as soon as the forty-minute practice ended. The doctor confirmed I was just bruised, and he wrapped my back and shoulder with ice. I sat in a chair and tried to get comfortable with the three packs freezing me through my T-shirt.

Josh came in with fruit from the hospitality room, and he handed me a banana as he sat beside me. "To hold you over until we can get lunch."

"Thanks." I shifted to find a better position. "This ice is not nearly as fun as ours was yesterday."

"Court!" Liza cried as she rushed into the room. "I read what happened on Twitter."

Sergei's nineteen-year-old daughter was one of my closest friends since she lived part-time with Em and Sergei and trained at our rink. As the three-time national champion and reigning world champion, she was the face of Team USA. Josh and I were under pressure to skate well, but it was nothing compared to the expectations on Liza's petite shoulders.

"I thought your dad told you to stay off Twitter," I said.

"I just took a little peek. Don't tell him." She lifted her finger to her lips. "So, you're okay?"

"Yeah, I'm just gonna look like I'm in a fight club. The ice is supposed to help, but I know how badly I bruise."

"I remember when you got hit with the volleyball at the beach last summer. Your arm was like Barney purple," Liza said.

"Then your skin will match your dress tomorrow. No one will even notice." Josh rubbed my arm.

I laughed a little. "I love your silver linings."

"You better be careful from now on." Liza's deep blue eyes crinkled with concern. "Don't forget the Sochi Pact."

"What's the Sochi Pact?" Josh asked.

"That we'll be roomies in the Village and compete in the team event," I said.

The new figure skating team event had everyone excited

because Team USA had a good chance to win a medal. If all the power players like Liza made it to Sochi, we would be strong in the men's, ladies, and dance events. Pairs was the biggest question mark. Josh and I weren't contenders for the podium in our individual competition, but if we were part of the team event I knew we could contribute solid points. It was something I'd tried not to think about too much — the possibility of winning an Olympic medal. I needed to stay focused on just making the team.

Liza's phone beeped, and she glanced at the notification. "Kristin's waiting for me upstairs. I came over here to meet with a sponsor."

"Give her my apologies again for my mom's unreasonable demands last night," Josh said.

"My mom is a handful, but yours is in her own category." Liza leaned over and gave me a gentle hug. "Take it easy. I'll check in later."

She hurried out as quickly as she'd come in, and I tore at the banana peel, careful not to mess up the manicure I'd gotten the previous afternoon.

"How do I get in on this pact?" Josh asked before he popped a grape into his mouth.

I patted his thigh. "You can't be our roommate, Babe."

"I can do everything else."

I smiled. "You're really already included because you're my partner. Everything I do counts for both of us since we're one entity."

He gazed at me with the love I'd become so accustomed to seeing but never grew tired of witnessing. Taking my hand, he laced our fingers together and kissed my knuckles.

"We are," he said. "An unstoppable, unbreakable entity."

I rested my cheek against the back of the chair and stared into his eyes, seeking the confidence that had slipped away from me the past two days. *An unstoppable entity*, I repeated to myself, but my crappy practices continued to fuel my doubt.

Unstoppable, I reminded myself again.

But I couldn't help but think, *Unless I do something stupid to screw it all up.*

CHAPTER FOUR

MY HEAVY EYELIDS STRUGGLED TO RISE as Josh's cheerful phone alarm sang louder and louder. I'd stared at the ceiling most of the night until I'd finally fallen asleep just a few hours ago.

Today is the day.

Short program day.

My stomach flip-flopped, anticipating the competition that was still hours away. Josh shut off the alarm, and he settled back beside me and kissed my mess of curls.

"How do you feel?" he asked.

I scooted upright against the pillows, and my ribs responded with a dull ache. "A little sore."

Josh reached over to the nightstand and flipped on the lamp, and I turned sideways and pulled off my T-shirt.

"How does my back look?"

His hesitance to answer didn't give me a good feeling. I looked over my shoulder at him, and his eyes were pained at what he saw.

"That bad?" I said quietly.

His fingertips grazed my skin, and he touched his lips to my shoulder. "I hate seeing you hurt."

"It probably looks worse than it feels."

"Still… I wish I could've done something to stop you from falling."

I slipped my shirt over my head. "There was nothing you could do. Our momentum was going in opposite directions."

He rubbed his hand softly up and down my spine. "You think you'll be able to cover the bruises with makeup?"

"I hope so. Em said she'd come over to help me this afternoon."

Josh gave my waist a squeeze and picked up the menu from the nightstand as he climbed off the bed. "Want to order breakfast in?"

"Sure. I need coffee from downstairs, though." I went over to my suitcase. "You want me to get you anything?"

"Nah, I'll just have juice." He reached for the phone. "Egg white omelet with spinach, tomatoes, and peppers and a side of fruit?"

I loved that he knew my favorite breakfast, but my jittery stomach wasn't feeling the love. I had to make a good effort to eat, though, so I wouldn't pass out during the warm-up later.

"Perfect," I said with a forced smile.

I swapped my pajama pants for yoga pants, and I covered my T-shirt with a hoodie and my hair with a baseball cap. No one could fault me for looking like a bum before I'd had my Starbucks.

Down in the lobby the line stretched out the door of the coffee shop. I shuffled to the end of it and covered my mouth as I let out a huge yawn.

"Trouble sleeping last night? Me too," a twangy voice behind me said.

I groaned inside and slowly pivoted toward Roxanne. Her dark hair was piled atop her head in the biggest top knot I'd ever seen, and she was in full makeup as if she was about to skate.

"Big day," I said and faced the counter again.

"I'm glad Evan and I are skating in the last group so I can take a long nap later," she continued to talk even though I thought I'd given the clear vibe of *It's way too early to chit chat.*

"The crowd is always the best for the last group, too," she went on, and I felt obligated to halfway slant in her direction. "Though I'm sure it'll be great when you and Josh skate early. You have the whole city behind you."

I stifled another yawn. "We need all the support we can get. I know better than anyone how hard it is to make the team."

"I keep forgetting you haven't been to the Olympics yet. Probably because you're all over the ads everywhere." Her gray eyes flashed with irritation.

Ahh, yes, I should've known she'd go there again. Ever since Josh and I had been invited to the Olympic media summit where we'd posed for sponsors, Roxanne had made comments hinting she and Evan had been slighted. As if Josh and I had any control over who the federation had chosen to represent Team USA at the event.

Thankfully, the clerk beckoned me forward, so I had an excuse to ignore Roxanne's complaining. After I ordered my latte with soy milk, I stood in the middle of the crowd to keep Roxanne at bay. I managed to get my drink and exit the shop without any more conversation, but I stopped short as I approached the elevators. Josh's mom was coming straight for me.

What is this? Run-into-every-annoying-person morning?

"Courtney, I was hoping to see you. I need a few words with you," Mrs. Tucker said.

"My breakfast is waiting upstairs, so…" I made a move for the elevator.

"This will only take a few minutes." She touched my elbow and urged me toward a table outside the café.

I lowered the brim of my cap and sank onto one of the chairs. The less eye contact I made with Mrs. Tucker the better.

I couldn't imagine this being a pleasant conversation. It never was with her.

"Your practices have left a lot to be desired, wouldn't you say?" she began.

I winced at the direct hit, but I should've expected it. She never was one to beat around the bush.

"Luckily, practices don't count," I said.

I kept my head down, but I couldn't escape the coldness of her glare. I wrapped my hands around my cup to draw upon its warmth.

"No, but the short program does count, and you can't afford to make any mistakes. You have to put yourself in position to win on Saturday."

"I'm well aware of that." I tried to keep my voice even.

"I'm just making sure you realize how important this is. You already ruined Josh's life once. You'd better not ruin this for him, too."

My knuckles strained around my drink, and I gritted my teeth, not allowing my exhaustion to override good sense. Her words had stabbed at the heart of my anxiety, but going off on Josh's mom in the middle of the hotel lobby wasn't how I should start my day. She had no idea how important this competition was to me. It was *too* important. I shoved back my chair and shot to my feet.

"I have to go."

I punched the elevator button and ducked into the corner of the empty car. My anxiousness rose as quickly as the floor numbers.

Of course I didn't want to mess this up for Josh. I didn't want to mess this up for *us*. No matter how many times I told myself not to get caught up in the Olympic dream again, I couldn't stop the madness. I wanted us to make the team so badly I'd been crippling myself with fear on the ice. Fear that once again I wasn't going to succeed, but this time it would hurt even worse because I'd be letting Josh down, too. My best friend and the love of my life.

The elevator opened, and I slowly made my way to the room. When I reached the door, I paused for a few calming breaths. I didn't want Josh to see me rattled and to know his mom had confronted me. It would just upset him, and he didn't need that today.

Short program day.

I took a swig of coffee, hoping to drown the edgy flutters, and I slid my key into the door.

A FEW HOURS AND one shaky twenty-minute warm-up later, I stood at the bathroom counter, arranging and rearranging my makeup and hair products. Each of my fingers had developed a nervous tic and wouldn't stop moving.

Josh shrugged on his team jacket as he stepped into the doorway. He was going to hang out with Stephanie while Em helped me get ready.

"Text me when you're done?" he said.

"Sounds good," I said, fumbling two tubes of lipstick.

"Hey." He moved behind me and circled his arms around my shoulders, and I looked up at our reflection in the mirror.

"We're going to be great tonight." He held my gaze and didn't blink. "I can feel it."

I leaned back into him and let his strong arms surround me with positivity. Oh, how I wanted to feel it, too. But all I felt was overwhelming terror.

A knock on the door took Josh's warm embrace away from me. Em's voice carried into the room, and she bid Josh goodbye before joining me at the sink.

"This feels very familiar," she said.

I dropped my eyeliner and crouched to the tile to pick it up. "Huh?"

"Your first nationals. I did your makeup and hair for

you?"

"Oh… yeah. Lots of déjà vu happening this week."

Another knock came on the door, and I scrunched my eyebrows. "Who could that be?"

"I'll get it," Em said.

My chest seized with alarm. "Wait! If it's Josh's mom, tell her I'm busy."

"Don't worry. She won't get past me."

Em looked through the peephole and smiled. I ventured out beside her, and she opened the door to reveal a bellman holding a crystal vase full of purple roses.

"I have these for Courtney Carlton," he said.

"That's me." I lifted my hand, and he presented me with the bouquet. "Hang on just a sec."

I went to get my purse, but Em paid the tip before I could retrieve my wallet.

"Thanks," I said as I set the vase on the desk.

"These are gorgeous." She fingered one of the delicate petals. "They're the exact color of your costume."

I opened the large card included with the bouquet and recognized the handwriting. "They're from Josh."

"Like there was any question." Em smiled.

Holding the card firmly in my shaky hands, I read silently.

The purple rose symbolizes enchantment, and that is what I felt the very first time I saw you and what I still feel every moment I'm with you. I am in constant awe of your beauty and your strength. It is the ultimate honor for me to skate with you, and I can't wait to step on the ice with you tonight.

I love you,

Josh

With my emotions already at level-ten crazy, I couldn't hold back the tears. I let out a strangled cry and dropped onto the edge of the bed.

"Court." Em's eyes grew big, and she sat beside me.

"What... is it the note?"

I shook my head because my throat was too tight to speak. The note wasn't the issue. It had just magnified how much I loved Josh and wanted to fulfill my dream with him. The issue was the lifetime of skating I'd spent trying to reach the holy grail of competitions and the smothering feeling of dread I had about taking the ice.

"I knew this was going to happen," I choked out. "Four years ago I thought I made peace with not making the team, and skating with Josh was just going to be about having fun and trying new things and doing what I love most with the person I love most. But the closer we got to this season, the more I started fixating on the Olympics again, and as badly as I wanted to make the team in the past, I want it even more this time because it's *Josh*. And experiencing it with him would be so incredible my heart can't even take it."

I gasped for breath, and Em brought me into her arms. She didn't say anything as she let me cry all the tears I needed to release. I'd been holding in all these thoughts and feelings, not wanting to admit how freaked out I was.

When I had a handle on myself, I pulled back and wiped my wet face with my palms. "I'm sorry I'm such a mess. You probably thought I'd be more together this time since I've gone through this twice before."

She squeezed my knee. "As someone who spent the entire 2006 season having panic attacks, I'm in no position to judge. I know what it's like to be obsessed with the idea of something and to want it so much you make yourself crazy."

"The thing is, I don't just want it for myself. Even though Josh has already been to the Olympics, I know how special going with me would be for him. There's a reason he saved his favorite piece of music for this season. It's always been on his mind. It's always been what he's dreamed about. And I'm terrified I'm going to screw up and ruin everything."

Em hugged me again and then stood and took my hands.

"Let's start getting you ready, and we'll talk about this."

She handed me my face wash, and I scrubbed the tear stains from my cheeks. As I blotted my face with a towel, Em uncapped the bottle of body makeup.

"Do you know how jealous I am of you and Josh?" she said.

I paused and looked at her curiously over the towel. Em had Sergei, who pretty much worshipped her, and she had an Olympic gold medal. What could Josh and I have that she was missing?

"I'm sure you understand my confusion," I said.

She faced me away from her, and I watched in the mirror as she moved the strap of my camisole aside and dabbed a spot of foundation on my back. The liquid felt cold and creamy.

"I adore Chris and wouldn't change one day of our partnership, but competing with Sergei, being able to skate with him every day... that's a little fantasy I'll always have. The times we skate together for fun at the rink are so magical." She smoothed her fingers in circles over my skin. "And you and Josh get to experience that all the time."

I gave her a little smile. "It is pretty great."

"Sure, rub it in." She poked my shoulder but smiled back. "My point in telling you this is I want you to realize there's no reason to be afraid tonight. Just look at Josh and remember why you agreed to skate with him four years ago. Not for medals or to go to the Olympics but to have that amazing feeling you get every time you're together on the ice."

I closed my eyes and pictured Josh standing next to me, holding my hand as we prepared to skate. It didn't matter how many years we'd been partners. I still felt an undeniable spark when we glided across the ice. The way he looked at me when we were skating together — it was like I was the greatest gift he could ever receive. He made me feel so special.

"You're right," I whispered and turned to Em. "I am *so*

lucky."

"And so is Josh." She touched my cheek. "Keep those thoughts in your mind and in your heart tonight, and let your body do what it's so well trained to do."

I nodded slowly, and Em resumed working on me. My body hadn't cooperated the past two days at practice, but I had to forget that. I'd spent hundreds of days at home doing perfect programs, and those were what mattered most.

Trust your body.
Trust your heart.
Let your beauty and your strength shine.

THE LOVELY STRAINS OF "Clair de Lune" usually put me in a serene frame of mind, but hearing the music in the distance on the TD Garden sound system amped up all my jitters. Josh and I were next to skate after the "Clair de Lune" pair, so we only had about five minutes until our blades would touch the ice.

Josh stood quietly beside me, moving his hands every so often as he mentally ran through our choreography. He liked to stay to himself until just a few moments before we had to report to the ice. Completely the opposite of him, I was bouncing around, talking to Em and Sergei about anything and everything to ward off any negative thoughts.

Josh stopped moving and sent me a smile, and I noticed a shiny spot on his forehead.

"Em, quick, you have my makeup?" I said.

She produced it in seconds, and I tapped the brush in the powder and fluffed it over Josh's face.

"Am I pretty now?" he asked.

I handed the supplies to Em and brushed a few powder particles from Josh's black shirt. Purple stones lined his deep V-neck and the edges of his sleeves, giving him the perfect amount of bedazzled sexiness.

"You're so pretty it hurts," I said.

He grinned and stepped closer to me so we were just a breath apart. Em and Sergei backed away, giving us space for our final moment together.

"I still pinch myself every time we compete because I can't believe I'm really skating with you." He traced his fingertips lightly under my jaw. "My dream girl."

I wrapped my arms around his waist and placed a whisper of a kiss on his lips. "It's all been real, but it's felt like a dream."

"And it's far from over," he said. "I'm counting the seconds until I can get out there and skate this hot flamenco program with you."

The huskiness of his voice sent a shiver through me, and I just about forgot the magnitude of the event. Sergei broke the spell when he cleared his throat.

"Time to go," he said.

The four of us walked through the tunnel and waited as the previous team spun into their ending pose. I took off my jacket, and Em gave my back a once-over for any makeup smudges. Josh pulled me into one more hug, and we stayed in the embrace until we received the signal to take the ice.

As soon as we removed our guards, the audience erupted with cheers. Goosebumps shot up all over my skin, and my heart thumped hard against my chest. I pushed off from the boards and took long, deliberate strokes.

While the score was read, Josh skated to my side and grasped my hand, and we glided over to Em and Sergei. The crowd had quieted for the score, but was now in full frenzy mode, yelling and waving signs of support. I took a tiny sip of water to wet my dry mouth, and I intertwined my fingers with Josh's, holding on as tightly as I could.

Sergei leaned forward so we could hear him over the chaos. "You have a connection no other team has. Focus on each other, and you'll make it all happen."

Josh and I bobbed our heads and skated to the end of the rink for our introduction. The booming cheers drowned out the pounding of my pulse in my ears. I looked up at Josh, and he squeezed my hand and mouthed, "I love you."

I smiled and exhaled the long breath I'd been holding.

Here we go.

CHAPTER FIVE

SURROUNDED ON ALL SIDES BY OVERWHELMING love from the crowd, Josh and I skated to center ice and tensed our bodies for our opening pose. Josh stood behind me, and we turned our heads slightly toward each other without making eye contact. I wished I could see the sureness in his eyes one last time, but I couldn't budge with the music about to start any second.

The quick strum of the guitar began, and I remembered the advice Em had given me at the hotel. Josh stroked my arm, sparking the fire inside me, and I zeroed all my focus on the heat and the energy between us.

Our eyes met as we took our initial steps across the ice, and I saw how intensely Josh was locked in on me. With the strong guitar beat guiding us, I felt completely inside the program already. Josh reached for my hand, and we sped toward the triple twist, our blades whooshing in unison.

I drifted closer to him, gliding on a back outside edge, and he clutched my hips and rocketed me into the air. I stretched my legs into a split and then quickly pulled my body into a tight coil, twisting three times. As I came down from my high, Josh caught my waist and returned my feet effortlessly to the ice. The audience's cheers sounded far away as I kept my eyes on Josh's, continuing to live in the little world of just the two of us.

We had to turn away from each other to set up for the side-by-side triple Salchows, and I felt the connection to Josh slip away. My heart raced in double time as a blast of reality hit me. I hadn't landed a clean Salchow all week.

You have to get this. You HAVE to make this happen.

We curved toward the judges, and I fought against the panic seizing my muscles. Pushing off from the ice, I spun three times, but the ground was coming too fast. I hadn't jumped high enough. My right blade hit before I could open up for the landing, and my stomach dropped as I felt myself leaning off balance. I splayed my arms wide, but I couldn't stop myself from falling.

Oh God, this isn't happening.

A hush fell over the crowd, followed quickly by applause of encouragement. The sting of the ice made me bounce right back up, and I looked to Josh, who was perfectly upright and holding his hand out toward me.

"Stay with me," he said.

I took his hand and refocused on the determination in his eyes. We were at a critical moment, where I could either let the mistake shake me or I could blow past it as if it had never happened. Our dream was hanging off the edge of a cliff by its fingernails.

I knew exactly what I had to do.

I had to *fight, fight, fight* every second for the rest of the program.

With the fire back in my step, I followed Josh's lead into our footwork sequence. We mirrored each other's steps with crispness and ease, giving every movement the fierceness Em and Sergei had taught us. We finished with a tight set of twizzles and then powered forward to the setup for the throw triple flip.

Josh moved behind me, and we sailed backward in a straight line, his hands on my hips. I felt his strength in the curl of his fingertips, and I felt my own deep within. I jabbed my right toe pick into the ice, and Josh winged me into the air. Three turns later, I came down with a clean landing, not a spray of ice to be found.

The music slowed a bit, and we whirled into our side-by-side spins. Since I had the louder voice of the two of us, I was in charge of calling out "Change!" when we had to switch positions during the spins. Josh heard my cues, and we stayed exactly in sync through each variation. The crowd suddenly sounded louder as we regained speed and stroked around the corner of the rink.

Josh swung me up over his head, and I got a clear view of the fans beating their hands together for us. All the faces whizzed past me and then turned upside down as I twisted backward in the lift. Josh held me up by just my hip as he rotated over the ice, his feet turning swiftly and smoothly, and a roar went up when I flipped over for the set down.

I pressed my palm to Josh's chest, and his heartbeat pounded in time with mine. We shared a lingering, smoldering look, and I arched my back and pivoted down into our last element, the death spiral. As I rose to my feet, Josh hooked his arm around my waist, and we stood nose to nose, our lips so close to touching. The final notes of "Nyah" trailed away.

Josh gazed into my eyes and didn't let me go even as the audience showered us with applause. So much adrenaline was still coursing through me, and I leaned into Josh and kissed him. He wrapped me in a hug, and as I slowly caught my breath, the magic faded and a heavy weight sank upon me. The performance had been strong, but I'd made an error that would definitely cost us.

We bowed to all four sides of the arena and skated to the

boards hand in hand. Em gave us a smile, but I saw the worry behind it.

"I'm so proud of you," she said as she embraced me. "You fought back so hard."

Sergei said the same as we hugged and stepped up into the kiss and cry. He and Em flanked Josh and me on the short bench, and I watched my failed jump replay in slow motion on the monitor in front of us. My hands balled into fists.

That damn Salchow.

Josh touched the small of my back and bent his head to my ear. "Jump or no jump, we killed that program."

The monitor showed a close-up of us during the footwork, playing off each other with flirtatious smiles. Had we dazzled the judges enough to keep us in the running for the top two spots? Since we'd skated in an early group, we were going to have to wait over an hour for the final result.

"The score for Courtney Carlton and Joshua Tucker," the announcer began.

I dug my nails into Josh's thigh and stared at the TV screen. *Please don't bury us.*

"The score for their short program — sixty-five point two five. They are currently in first place."

Sergei patted my knee, and I let out a tiny exhale. Considering the huge mistake I'd made, the score was pretty good. But none of the major contenders had skated yet, so we likely wouldn't be in first place for long.

We moved backstage for a series of interviews, and by the time we finished we'd been bumped down to third place. We changed out of our costumes and went upstairs to watch the final group, specifically Roxanne and Evan.

As we got quick hugs from my parents on the concourse, a horde of fans approached us for pictures and autographs. I appreciated their support, but I was having trouble putting on a genuine smile. Inside I was only getting angrier with myself for letting nerves overpower me on the jump. No way could that happen again. We were in a situation where we had to skate perfectly in the free skate to have any chance of moving up.

"Steph's in Section Twenty-Two," Josh said as he looked at his phone. "She said she's by herself. My parents are somewhere else."

That was all I needed to hear to follow him to her seat. Stephanie might not be the most sympathetic person regarding my mistake on the ice, but she wouldn't berate me like Mrs. Tucker would. I couldn't avoid Josh's mom forever, but I was going to stall as long as possible.

Stephanie waved us into two empty seats beside her, and she gave us both hugs, mine more a courtesy.

"Well, your dress looked fabulous," she said. "I hope you'll get a chance to wear it again."

The slight snarkiness to her tone actually made me smile. Stephanie had come a long way in accepting me as Josh's girlfriend and partner, but she couldn't stop the attitude from coming out every now and then.

"Did you ditch Mom and Dad?" Josh asked.

"They were arguing about dinner later, and I was so over it. It's no wonder they couldn't agree since they barely talk to each other."

Her mouth turned down, and I thought about my own parents and how easy their relationship was. They didn't lead an exciting life like the Tuckers did, but they enjoyed each other's company and hardly ever fought. I had the total opposite from Josh in parental role models.

The six-minute warm-up on the ice ended, and we all put our attention on Roxanne and Evan striking their opening pose. For two-and-a-half minutes I watched them conquer each element, though not with the expert unison Josh and I had shown. They finished with their arms open to the audience and huge smiles on their faces, and the uneasiness in my stomach grew as I added up the points in my head. Their score was going to be massive.

I couldn't stand to look as the numbers came up on the video board. I didn't have to because Roxanne's shrieking and fist pumping told me the story. They were seven points ahead of us.

"She needs to calm the hell down." Stephanie glared at the kiss and cry.

Even in her bratty days, Stephanie hadn't ever made a spectacle of herself when the score was announced. Roxanne was acting like the competition was over.

"Anything can happen in the long," Josh said.

"Exactly," Stephanie said. "You can make up seven points. They're going to crash and burn on the quad, and there's nothing special about the rest of their skating."

The next team took the ice, so the conversation halted, but I kept silently running the numbers, thinking back to our season's best score versus Roxanne and Evan's. We'd topped them by seven points before, so doing it again was very possible. We only had to finish second to make the Olympic team, but I really wanted to win on our home turf and prove we were worthy of all the attention we'd received.

And I didn't want that one stupid jump to be the reason we lost the title.

The remaining three teams didn't crack into the top of the standings, so we were still in fourth place when the final leaderboard flashed on the screen. Josh and I headed back downstairs to draw for the free skate start order, and he pulled me aside before we reached the media room.

"You've been so quiet," he said. "Don't keep beating yourself up over the Sal."

"It's just so freaking frustrating. Everything else was the best we've ever done. If I'd landed it, we'd be in first for sure."

"We're still in this. We just need to start with a clean slate at practice tomorrow. Today is done and all that matters is getting ready for Saturday." He gently squeezed my shoulders. "Are you with me?"

I flashed back to our performance and the similar pivotal point I'd encountered when my butt had hit the ice. I'd made the right decision then and I had to do the same now. I had to stomp out the regret and only look forward. It was the only way we'd have any chance for greatness.

"Always," I said.

He hugged me to his side and kissed the top of my head as we entered the room where all the other pairs had gathered. We would be in the final flight of four teams on Saturday, so we had to wait until almost the end to pick our start order number. Josh had drawn the optimal last spot four years ago for Stephanie and him, so I let him try to replicate that when our names were called. He rubbed his hands together and reached inside the bag, and I crossed my fingers and watched his face for his reaction.

He smiled.

YES.

He held up the number, which represented the final spot in the order. We would close out the event and leave the lasting impression on the judges, and the crowd would be totally worked up and ready to explode by that point. It was all set up for us to have our shining moment.

We just had to deliver.

CHAPTER SIX

WITH THE TEMPERATURE NO LONGER AT brutally-cold level, Josh and I decided to walk from the arena to the nearby North End for dinner. Stephanie joined us but was on her phone with a work issue during the half-mile trek to Boston's neighborhood of all things Italian.

I wheeled my skate bag across Salem Street and stopped in front of L'Osteria on the corner. I'd eaten there a few times and knew it would have vegan options for Stephanie.

"Is this place okay?" I asked her as I pointed to the menu next to the door.

She paused her conversation and took a quick glance. After a nod of approval we all went inside, where the stark contrasting warmth had me tearing off my coat. We sat beside the windows, Josh and I on one side of the table and Stephanie on the other.

"You'd think I'm the boss and not the intern," she said as she placed her phone on the table. "The assistant to the designer I'm working for is so clueless. I don't know how this guy finds his way to the office every day."

A tall, dark-haired waiter who looked like he'd just

arrived straight from Italy stepped up to our table, and Stephanie's snarl quickly turned into a smile. We gave our drink orders, and her eyes followed the waiter as he retreated to the kitchen.

"Excellent restaurant choice," she said.

I laughed and unfolded my napkin. Stephanie's phone vibrated on the white tablecloth, and she picked it up, read the message, and slapped it face down.

"I will be so glad when I'm done with this job and this idiot."

"Are you still thinking of moving to New York after graduation?" Josh asked.

"Depends who gives me the best offer. I feel like I should probably experience the scene in New York for a few years, though."

"If you want to do more costume design, you'll have a ton of customers," I said. "Everyone has been raving about the ones you made for us."

"Wait until they see your exhibition dress." She paused and flashed a smile at the waiter as he set down her glass of red wine. "I impressed even myself with that one."

"When Court tried it on to show me, I had no words," Josh said.

I grinned and brushed my leg against his. He'd had no words but he'd said plenty in the hot way he'd looked at me and touched me as he'd helped me out of the dress. I'd chosen pink because I was wearing that color the first time Josh saw me skate, and our exhibition program was about the unlikely journey we'd traveled since that moment. I just hoped when we debuted it Sunday after the competition, it would be a triumphant performance and not a sorrowful one.

"Oh, hell," Stephanie said as she gazed out the window.

I curved my neck to see the problem and found it in the form of Mr. and Mrs. Tucker on the sidewalk. They'd spotted us and were now entering the restaurant. I prayed for a trap door to open under my feet. Rehashing the short program was *not* what I felt like doing.

"I tried calling both of you." Mrs. Tucker eyed Stephanie and Josh as she cast her dark shadow over the table.

"I was dealing with work stuff," Stephanie said.

Josh offered no explanation. I was sure he'd chosen to ignore his mom's calls.

"Can you put our tables together?" Mrs. Tucker asked the hostess.

"There's not much space," Josh argued, but the hostess had already begun scurrying under Mrs. Tucker's sharp stare.

The waiter returned to take our dinner orders, and I longed for him to stay. Not because he was good-looking, but so he could distract Mrs. Tucker from bringing up my miscue on the ice. Stephanie helped the cause, laughing and flipping her long, brown hair over her shoulder as she discussed vegan ingredients with him.

"So, fourth place," Mrs. Tucker said as soon as the waiter left.

"Yes, and looking forward to the free skate," Josh jumped in with no hesitation. "We've already put today behind us, so we don't need any more discussion on it."

"Well, I suppose that's the only attitude you can have right now considering…" She sent me a cool sidelong glance past Josh, who sat between us.

I took a long drink of water and noticed Mr. Tucker typing on his phone as usual. He might've been completely out of touch with his family, but I'd take that over his wife's sudden meddling in our business.

"Are you coming to Sochi with us?" Mrs. Tucker asked Stephanie. "*If* we have a reason to go."

Josh's hand clenched around his glass, and I touched his thigh under the table.

"I told you I'm not," Stephanie said. "I can't take more time away from school and work."

Mrs. Tucker hummed quietly. "We have a large suite on the sea, so if you change your mind we have plenty of room."

"What are the dates again?" Mr. Tucker finally put his attention on the humans around him instead of the object in his hand. "Second week of February?"

"The Opening Ceremony is the seventh," I said before anyone else could answer. I'd memorized all the key dates:

Team Event Short Program — February Sixth

Team Event Free Skate — February Eighth

Pairs Event Short Program — February Eleventh

Pairs Event Free Skate — February Twelfth

Mr. Tucker stared at me for a second as if what I'd said didn't make sense, and then he turned to Mrs. Tucker. "I have a conference in Napa that weekend."

She plunked her wine glass down hard. "I told Christy to put the trip on your calendar."

"I don't see it." He scrolled on his phone.

"I'm sure you can skip the conference."

He looked up, his light eyes solidly fixed on his wife. "No. I can't."

"You've known all along we would be going to Sochi in February." Mrs. Tucker's tone harshened further. "You should've checked with me before you booked this conference."

"Maybe if you actually talked to each other instead of communicating through Dad's secretary, you wouldn't have these problems," Stephanie snapped.

My eyebrows shot up, and I tapped the floor, wishing for that trap door again. Just when I'd thought the dinner couldn't be any more uncomfortable, I got to sit in the middle of the Tucker Family Bicker Hour.

"You should ask one of your friends to go with you," Mr. Tucker said.

"One of my friends?" Mrs. Tucker spat out. "You need to be there representing the family with me."

Oh my God. They're fighting over a trip that could possibly not even happen.

I massaged my temples. *That's not positive thinking,* I reminded myself, but I had to keep it real.

"I need to be in Napa growing my business. The one that's paying for this luxury suite in Russia." Mr. Tucker swirled his wine and downed all of it.

Josh pushed his hand through his hair. "Can we please talk about something else or not talk at all? We're trying to stay focused on one event at a time, that being our long program in two days. Nothing else."

Mrs. Tucker was still glaring at her husband. "We'll discuss the trip later."

"There's nothing more to discuss," he fired back.

Stephanie groaned and threw her napkin on the table. "I'm going to the ladies' room."

"I think I'll join you," I said, seeking at least a momentary escape.

When we emerged at the sinks a few minutes later, Stephanie scrubbed her hands together and pounded them dry with paper towels.

"I swear I'm never getting married," she said. "It's just misery waiting to happen."

"Not every couple is like that," I said.

"Most of the ones I've seen are," she said and swept out the door.

I stood there, slowly wiping my hands. Josh had grown up in the same dysfunctional environment as Stephanie, but I'd never thought he was jaded about marriage. With his silence on the topic lately, though, I had to wonder if all the dysfunction had affected him, too.

I crumpled the paper towel and tossed it into the trash, which was where I needed to put my worries, too. *All that should be on your mind is skating.*

THE CROWD ROARED, DROWNING out the music, and I shivered from the goosebumps covering my arms. The skating, the emotion, the atmosphere… everything had been perfect. It was exactly how I envisioned our final nationals performance.

"What are you watching?" Josh asked as he came out of the bathroom, his hair still glistening from the shower.

I propped up on my elbows and turned down the volume on my phone. "Em and Chris's nationals free skate here in 2001. It was one of the greatest skates I've ever seen and the most electric atmosphere I've ever experienced."

Josh sat on the end of the bed and peered at the tiny screen, where Sergei was hugging a sobbing Em.

"Were you crying in the stands?" He smiled.

"I was. I was bawling."

I actually had a little lump in my throat watching now and recalling the energy in the building that night.

"That can easily be us tomorrow afternoon," Josh said.

I stared at the video. Em and Chris's near-perfect scores came up, and they were both wide-eyed with shock and glee as they embraced in the kiss and cry. The announcer's voice couldn't be heard over the audience's screaming. God, I wanted that to be us tomorrow so badly.

"We've put in so much work, and I've come so close before." I looked up at Josh. "We have to get our storybook ending, right?"

"I believe what may seem like an impossible dream can very much come true. The fact that you're here with me right now is proof."

I smiled and soaked in the adoration in his eyes. There was never a second with Josh that I didn't feel loved. I kissed his arm and nuzzled my nose to his warm skin, and he bent and buried his lips in my hair.

"There's something I want to give you." He got up and

went to his suitcase. "I was going to wait until after we skated, but..."

My heart thundered as Josh dug under the clothes in his bag. *Is this the moment?* I scrambled to sit up, and I touched my ring finger. Would it no longer be empty in a few minutes?

Josh turned around with a flat, square something in his hands, and I almost laughed at how he kept unknowingly faking me out. He had no idea how much he was torturing me.

He returned to my side and handed me the wrapped gift. "I've had this for a long time, but I thought this weekend would be the perfect time to give it to you."

I tore away the gold paper and flipped over the picture frame. Two photos filled the front of the red frame. The one on the right I recognized immediately — a shot of Josh and me in our Team USA jackets at our first competition together. The picture on the left also showed us in our team jackets, but we were teenagers. It took me a few seconds to place the scene, and when I did I looked up at Josh with disbelief.

"How did you get this picture? And did you crop out the old lady?" I laughed.

"The day after we took it I—"

Josh's phone rang on the bed, and he leaned back to see the screen. "It's one of my students' moms. Sorry, I'd better get it."

"Yeah, go ahead."

While he answered the call, I gazed at the photo and smiled as memories of that morning at nationals in Atlanta ten years ago flooded over me.

"What do you want to do today to celebrate?" Mom asked as we finished breakfast in the hotel restaurant. "A national championship deserves something very special."

I smiled and drank the last of my chocolate milk. My partner Mark and I had finally reached the top of the podium, winning the junior title in pairs. It had been the highlight of my fifteen-year life.

"Maybe we can go shopping... and look at iPods?" I gave Mom

a hopeful grin.

"We might be able to do that."

I did a jig in my seat and folded my linen napkin. "I'm gonna get some more fruit."

I headed over to the buffet but stopped when I saw Josh Tucker, one of my competitors, looking at the fruit selection. He was a year older than me and SO freaking cute with his shaggy dark hair and clear blue eyes. But we'd hardly spoken since we'd played Seven Minutes in Heaven (or rather, Seven Minutes in Hell) two years ago. I'd wanted him to be my first kiss so badly, but all we'd shared were seven minutes of near silence. Even though Josh was a super quiet guy, I'd hoped he would make just a little move on me. I'd gotten nothing.

Normally I didn't go out of my way to talk to him because I still felt weird about that night, but I was feeling especially confident with my new champion status. I grabbed a small plate and hopped up to Josh's side.

"I'll fight you for that last piece of cantaloupe."

He looked startled, and he fumbled the silver tongs and dropped them on the bar, causing a loud clang. "You can umm... you can have it."

"I was just joking," I said with a little laugh.

He echoed my laugh but with a nervous edge. "I know, but you... it's yours."

He offered me the tongs, keeping his head down. I reached for them, and our fingers brushed, sparking tingles from my scalp to my toes. Josh finally looked up at me, for only a few seconds, but the light in his eyes was enough for the tingles to flush my cheeks.

"Thanks." I dipped my own head, suddenly not feeling so confident anymore.

"Excuse me." An older lady tapped the arm of Josh's Team USA jacket. "Can I get a picture with you and your partner?"

She motioned to me, and Josh and I both stammered while talking over each other.

"I'm not—"

"She's not—"

"I'm not his partner," I finished.

"Oh, sorry about that. Too many faces to keep straight," she said.

"We can still take a picture with you," Josh said.

I raised my eyebrows, but the lady was already handing her camera to the elderly man with her. Josh and I set down our plates, and I waited for the woman to stand between us, but Josh led her to his opposite side so he was in the middle.

Next to me.

He hesitated a moment and then stretched his arm across my shoulders. It was wiry but solid. I inched closer and curved mine around his waist, slotting perfectly into the nook of his body.

Holy Romeo, he smelled good.

The scent of his cologne was slightly sweet and made me light-headed. I barely registered the camera flash firing. I was too busy picturing Josh putting his other arm around me and giving me the kiss he owed me.

"Thank you, kids," the lady said.

Josh slowly let his arm fall away from my shoulders, and he shuffled backward and shoved his hands in his pockets.

"That was hilarious," he said. "I don't look anything like Mark."

"And I sure don't look like Stephanie," I said of his partner and sister. I was about to add, "Don't act like her either" because she was a first-class snob, but I stopped myself from being rude.

Josh's eyes focused on mine, and it felt as if he was saying something to me he couldn't say out loud. From the way he was looking at me, it had to be important. My pulse picked up more speed every second he waited to speak.

"Congratulations, by the way," he said.

That didn't seem like what he'd wanted to tell me, but I smiled anyway.

"Thanks. I saw you guys had a good comeback."

He shrugged and looked down at his sneakers. "It wasn't our

best competition."

"Josh!" Stephanie marched over to us and gave me a scowl. "What are you doing? We have to go."

"Oh… yeah… I forgot." He turned back to me. "We have a meeting."

My heart sank that he was leaving just as we'd actually started talking. Should I hint we could talk more later? How was I going to smoothly pull that off? And with Stephanie giving me the stink eye?

I chickened out and said quietly, "Have fun."

They walked away, and Josh glanced quickly at me over his shoulder. Stephanie didn't give me another look (nor had she congratulated me, but that didn't shock me). She was so easy to read. Unlike her brother.

I picked up my plate and plopped the slice of cantaloupe onto it. Standing so close to Josh had made me wonder for the millionth time what kissing him would've been like. He was so quiet and gentle that I imagined his kiss would be soft and sweet. The perfect first kiss. Not like the one my Homecoming date had given me. He'd practically cracked my teeth he'd crashed his mouth into mine so hard.

Why was I even still thinking about this? It had taken Josh and me two years to say more than five words to each other. At the rate we were going, we'd be thirty by the time we got to first base.

I laughed to myself as I remembered how frustrated I'd been. If only I'd known then how incredible our first kiss and every kiss after that would be. All the years of waiting had just made them sweeter.

Josh hung up his call and put the phone on the desk. "Sorry, it was a scheduling issue."

"That's okay. It gave me time to take a trip down memory lane."

"Before the phone rang, I was about to say I saw the lady at breakfast again the next day, and driven by my massive crush on you, I asked her if she'd send me a copy of the photo. I told her we were friends but didn't get to see each other much since we lived on opposite sides of the country. I'm not sure if she bought it or if she thought I was a total creeper." He laughed.

"That is amazing. I can't believe you've had this picture for ten years."

"I kept it in a safe place where Stephanie would never find it. Whenever I'd choreograph programs in my head and I'd imagine skating them with you, I'd look at it and remember how you felt next to me. I never gave up on the dream of having you that close to me again."

The lump returned to my throat, and I curled my fingers into Josh's hair. Who needed a ring when I had more love than I could ask for? I kissed his lips, smiling against them.

"Closer than you could've ever imagined," I said.

He grinned and smoothed his hands around my waist. "If I'd known at sixteen what we'd be doing now, I would've self-combusted."

I giggled. "So, why did you wait until now to show me the picture?"

"When we became partners I got the idea to pair it with our photo from our first event, and then I decided to wait and give it to you at our last nationals. I thought it was the perfect symbol of how far we've come and how anything is possible."

I picked up the frame and smiled as I looked again at the photos. "And you knew I needed that reminder now more than ever."

"Is it helping?" He hugged me against him with one arm.

I connected with his eyes and gave him another kiss, and then I slipped off the bed with the frame in hand. I placed it next to our Daruma on the nightstand and went back to Josh, straddling his legs so we sat face to face.

"I love all the symbols you've given me that remind me to have faith. It's been really hard for me to forget all the disappointment I've had, but I've realized one very important thing." I tugged lightly on his T-shirt. "You and I were always meant to be here, so the disappointment happened for a reason. And I know with all my heart that tomorrow we are going to do everything we can to make our dream come true."

CHAPTER SEVEN

BREATHE.

It was crazy I had to tell myself to do that basic function, but my nervous energy had thrown everything out of whack. Just seconds away from the six-minute warm-up, I stood in a crowd of my competitors, smothering from sparkles. I closed my eyes and shut out the noise and the shininess. Breathing slowly in and out, I concentrated on Josh's strong hands on my shoulders and the warmth of his presence behind me.

My eyes opened to see a TV camera pointed at my face, so I stared straight ahead at the ice. I couldn't think about the millions of people watching at home, wondering if I was going to finally reach my seemingly unreachable star.

"Would the following couples please take the ice..."

Josh and I were announced last since we were skating last, and the audience saved their loudest and longest cheers for us. We flew around the rink in our back crossover warm-up, weaving between the three other teams. Josh popped me into the air for our triple twist, and the cheers fired up even louder.

We slowed to find a pocket of space for our next element,

and I looked around us. In our teal costumes we stood out as a splash of color among all the black and white worn by the rest of the group. I knew our skating would stand out, too, as long as I found a way to land the triple Salchow, the jump I hadn't done cleanly all week.

Gliding on back edges, we slipped between two teams and completed a huge throw triple flip. I held the landing a few extra moments, branding the feeling of success in my mind. I needed to duplicate that feeling on the Salchow.

We skated past Em and Sergei, and their encouraging nods and smiles stayed with me as we built up speed for the side-by-side jumps. *They know you can do this. YOU know you can do this.*

I pushed off the ice and spun tightly in the air. All my muscles responded without any thinking on my part, and before I knew it my right blade had connected with the ice. My knee wobbled with excitement as I realized I'd conquered my nemesis, but I stayed upright.

Yes!

Josh was smiling beside me, and I put my hand in his with a flourish. We stroked along the edge of the rink and stopped in front of Em and Sergei. As we sipped from our water bottles, Sergei said, "That was perfect."

"I knew I could do it." I slapped the boards.

"And you'll do it again in the program," Em said. "Just as easily."

"Should we run through the toes next?" Josh asked.

Sergei nodded. "Then the loop."

We set our bottles on the boards and reentered the busy scene on the ice. When two other teams moved out to talk to their coaches, we took the opportunity to carve a path across the rink for our side-by-side triple toe-double toe combination. We picked into the ice and rotated in sync on both jumps, landing with matching clean edges. We followed that with a solid throw triple loop, and I was practically giddy. I wished we could skate first even though last was the premium spot. I didn't want to lose the empowered feeling I currently had while waiting for everyone else to skate.

As we closed in on the final seconds of the warm-up, we practiced one of our lifts and finished with our pair spin. The announcer directed, "Couples, please leave the ice," and I let everyone else go ahead of me through the door. I wanted to feel the ice under my feet as long as possible.

Josh and I snapped on our guards and followed Em and Sergei backstage to a tucked-away nook. Roxanne and Evan went in the opposite direction but not before Roxanne gave me one of her bug-eyed death stares she usually reserved for her partner. If she thought she was being intimidating she was wrong. She just looked ridiculous.

Em helped me into my jacket so I could stay warm, and I started my standard pacing routine. Josh stood in one spot, jiggling his arms and legs ever so slightly, as he lost himself in his thoughts.

I began visualizing our program, and I could hear the music of Muse as if there was a stereo in my head. The actual recording we were using for our free skate was very special. The Cape Cod Symphony had performed the piece for us with Josh accompanying them on piano. Not many skaters in the history of the sport could say they'd skated to their own musical performance. Since Josh had also choreographed the program, his creative touch was all over it.

When I'd mentally run through the whole program, I flexed my knees and turned to Em and Sergei. I had to start chatting before my mind went places it shouldn't go.

"I talked to Liza earlier, and she sounded a little shaky," I said.

"I could see her tightening up at practice yesterday." Sergei shook his head. "Even though she has a huge lead, she's worried about putting up a big score tonight. I keep telling her not to think about keeping pace with the Russian girls. Just skate."

"That's really the best advice for all of us." I smoothed my fingers over my braided bun. "Just skate."

"It's the only thing totally in your control," Em said.

"I remember you telling me that at my first nationals."

She smiled. "Some pearls of advice are timeless."

Had it really been thirteen years since I'd done this for the first time? I still felt like that twelve-year-old girl in these moments before taking the ice. So vulnerable and so terrified of making a mistake. Even though I had every intention of fighting my butt off the entire four minutes, ice was slippery and there were no guarantees of success. The perfect jumps I'd done in the warm-up seemed so long ago now.

"Just a few more minutes," Sergei said as he looked at his watch.

Josh and I didn't have to speak. We came together like magnets and put our arms around each other. Usually we shared a few words, but today our embrace spoke for us. We held on tight, giving each other the silent assurances that only our love could inspire.

When we finally let go, we began the slow walk to the ice. Every step we took raised my adrenaline level, and I felt like I had been plugged into an electrical socket when we stepped out of the tunnel. Roxanne and Evan were still skating, so we hung back and faced away from the ice to stay focused on ourselves. I couldn't help but hear the loud applause at the end of the program, though.

Em took my jacket, and I rubbed my bare arms and patted my legs. *Get me onto the ice. Let's do this.*

I kept my head down so I wouldn't see Roxanne's face, but I heard her squeal as she and Evan met their coaches at the door. A larger part of me tensed, and I hurried to take off my guards and set my blades to the ice.

Josh and I glided separately around the rink as Ellie Goulding's "Burn" played over the sound system. There was no way I wouldn't hear Roxanne and Evan's score when it was announced, no matter how hard I willed myself to tune it out. I just had to do my job and remember what Em and Sergei had preached.

Just skate.

The music quieted, and I quickened my strokes, knowing what was coming. The announcer read the score, the very *large* score, and the tightness in my stomach curled into knots.

Holy crap, they must've landed the quad and everything else.

I'd never expected to hear a number that big. It completely changed the game. We were down to fighting for second place and the one remaining spot on the team. My legs quivered, and I glanced at Josh as he skated to my side and took my hand.

He looked stunned, too.

Double holy crap.

His fingers squeezed mine with added pressure as he guided me over to Em and Sergei. At least they were still smiling and didn't seem fazed.

"Just like the warm-up," Em said. "Light and easy."

I closed my eyes and tried to believe it could be that simple. *Heart, please stop beating so fast. Be calm!*

The crowd was anything but calm. Their noise rang so loudly I couldn't hear what Sergei said as Josh and I skated away. I'd looked forward to feeding off the crazy energy, but it was just making me shakier. I didn't feel in control of my body. Not the optimal situation when about to start a four-minute program.

We moved into our opening pose, standing back to back at center ice, and my heart beat up into my throat. I took a long swallow, but I couldn't push down the panicky sensation.

You gotta get it together NOW.

Right on cue, "Exogenesis: Symphony Part 3" began, and I was thankful our choreography didn't start until a few beats into the song. I breathed along with the slow piano notes and then stretched my right arm out to the side. Josh mimicked me, and we joined hands and turned to skate side by side.

Our contemporary dance movement took us across the ice and into the triple twist, where Josh's normally steady hands fumbled my waist on the catch. I sucked in a breath and exhaled when he set me down. His face was frozen with surprise, and I knew he was thinking the same thing I was. If we couldn't execute our money element perfectly, how were we going to get through the hard stuff?

The hardest happened to be next, so I dialed up the image of the perfect Salchow I'd done in the warm-up. *Don't think. Just jump.*

My body had memorized how to do the Salchow, but my limbs were so freaking jittery. Josh and I spaced apart to prepare for the setup, and I struggled to gain control of my nerves. With a quick push off the edge of my left blade, I sprang upward and pulled my arms in to rotate. I immediately sensed myself off axis and tried to correct my position, but I landed with a forward tilt, all my momentum threatening to take me down in a face-plant. I quickly shot my hand out and palmed the ice to brace myself and keep my body upright.

Next to me Josh was doing the same thing, and I marveled at our unison even when making mistakes. I doubted the judges would be as impressed. We couldn't have any more glaring errors or—

STOP. You know what you have to do.

I thought of our Daruma and keeping our focus trained on a positive outcome. Regardless of how rattled we felt, we had to give every drop of effort we had in our bodies. There could be no regrets.

Josh angled into me as we glided on a deep curve, and I said, "We're in this."

He held my gaze and gave me a quick nod.

We only had a few seconds to set up for the throw triple flip, so I hurried to mentally turn the page. Josh assisted me into the air, and I came down unsteadily on my right blade. I still hadn't been able to shake the jitters, but I wasn't going to let them dominate me. I dug into the ice and rode the landing as if it had been the most awesomely-executed throw we'd ever done.

I wanted to settle into the beautiful choreography Josh had created, but my mind was motoring with thoughts of each upcoming element. I couldn't rely on my anxiety-riddled body to handle matters on its own. I was going to have to think and grit my way through everything.

We muscled through the side-by-side triple toe-double toe combination with sticky landings but no hands down, and we carried that success into our star lift. I breathed a little easier, knowing we were halfway home, but I couldn't let myself relax too much. Between two more lifts, we had another difficult throw ahead — the triple loop.

Our speed increased as we sailed through the carry lift, and Josh dropped me gently into his arms before setting my feet on the ice. His eyes held the same determination I felt, giving me an extra pump of confidence for the throw. He swung me down in a pull-through motion and then stepped behind me, holding my hips for the take-off. As he tossed me upward, I sensed I was leaning again, just like on the Salchow. A shot of fear hit me, and I fought to shift my weight to my right side as I twisted three times. When my blade connected with the ice, I stretched my arms out and clenched every muscle, willing myself not to fall over. The audience erupted with cheers, and I let out the long breath I hadn't realized I'd been holding.

We stroked past Em and Sergei, who clapped just as hard as the crowd, and we knocked out our final lift to even louder applause. The music slowed, nearing the end of the program, and Josh pulled me close for our last element, the pair combination spin. His hands spanned my waist, and I arched backward in a layback position. The bright lights above whirled in a blur as we etched circles onto the ice. We changed positions three times and finished with Josh standing behind me, his arms wrapped around my shoulders. The final, quiet orchestral beat echoed through the arena.

Everyone in the stands jumped up, and gifts of all shapes and sizes flew from their hands onto the ice. Josh pressed me to his chest, and tears stung my eyes. We hadn't been perfect, but we had gutted out every second of the program. We'd given it more than our all.

I spun around, and Josh bent his forehead to mine. Our heartbeats and our breathing slowed together.

"We fought for that," he said.

I touched his face with both hands, and he gave me a soft kiss. We had to take our bows, but I wanted to make this moment last just a little longer. Our fate was still very much uncertain, and this could be the last time we'd stand on competition ice together. The tears that had welled in my eyes trickled down my cheeks. How had four years passed so quickly?

Josh held fast to me, too, but we eventually stepped apart to acknowledge the crowd's love. As we skated to the boards, I picked up a huge stuffed Minnie Mouse and looked up into the seats. Quinn and Alex were standing at the bottom of an aisle, waving frantically at us. I nudged Josh, and we went over and swallowed them in a group hug.

"You got our Minnie!" Quinn said.

"I love her." I cradled the stuffie in my arms. "And I love you guys."

I blew them kisses as we headed for Em and Sergei, and Em embraced us before we could make it off the ice.

"That was the hardest program I've ever done," I said.

"I could see you struggling, but you didn't give in," Em said. "I've never been more proud of you."

The four of us crammed onto the blue bench in the kiss and cry, and I reached for the box of Puffs, so fittingly a sponsor of the event. I blotted my face with a tissue and stored it inside my fist. No doubt I was going to need it in a minute. Whether I'd be crying tears of joy or disappointment was the heavy question.

Josh slipped his fingers between mine, and I rested my head on his shoulder. I didn't know how anyone other than Roxanne and Evan had skated, so anything could happen. My pulse had come down after our performance but was off to the races again. I'd suffered through this torturous wait so many times in my career, but it had never been as agonizing as this.

"And now the scores for Courtney Carlton and Joshua Tucker."

I lifted my head, and Sergei laid his arm across my shoulders and patted Josh on the back. My heart threatened to beat right out of my chest.

"The factored score for their free skate — one hundred thirty-three point two four."

A few random screams punctuated the silence, and I looked around at the crowd. Had some of our fans done the math already? Or were those screams for another team?

"Their total score — one hundred ninety-eight point four nine."

I stopped breathing. Was it enough? Had we done it?

"They are currently in second place."

The building exploded with a deafening roar and Josh yelled, "YES!" louder than I'd ever heard him speak.

He threw himself around me, and I tried to find my voice, but all that came out was a squeak. I was too shocked to move, to cry, to smile. There was so much noise and pandemonium around me, but everything inside me was eerily still and quiet. I couldn't believe I'd finally done it.

I was on the Olympic team.

Josh pulled back and locked his eyes on mine. "We're going to Sochi, Court."

I nodded weakly and whispered, "This is really

happening?"

He grinned and pressed our lips together, and I felt the realness in the joy of his kiss. A cry of elation broke through my shock and burst from my mouth.

Em and Sergei were standing and embracing each other, and I hopped up to hug both of them. One look at their wet eyes was all I needed to fall apart. My laughter became tears, and I clung to the two people who had been by my side from the beginning. I'd spent more time with them than my own family, and they'd taught me just as much about life and love as they had about skating. I could never thank them enough for all they'd given me.

"It's been a long road." Sergei's voice wavered. "And you've made us proud every step of the way."

"I love you both so much," I croaked.

Em sniffled. "We love you, too."

Josh joined our group lovefest, and we continued it backstage. Congratulations poured in from our competitors, the last being a half-hearted attempt from Roxanne. Her words didn't exactly match the disappointment on her face. I was flying too high to let her annoy me, but what was her problem? Wasn't it enough that they had beaten us?

My cheeks hurt from smiling as we answered questions and posed for photos at the press conference. Our official appointment to the Olympic team wouldn't come until tomorrow after the federation held its selection meeting, but we'd proven ourselves enough internationally the past few years to know we were a lock.

We had to wait for the ice dance event to conclude before our medal ceremony could begin, so I finally had a chance to check my phone. I skimmed through the multitude of texts and missed calls and saw one I needed to return immediately.

Liza picked up after one ring. "You're in!" she shouted.

"Sochi Pact, baby!"

"Oh my God, I thought I was going to have a nervous

breakdown when you were skating. I was literally checking my phone up until the second I had to get on the ice for my warm-up at the convention center. Every time you landed something, Chris would text me 'YES,' and when he wrote 'second place' I started jumping up and down."

I laughed. "Did you have a good warm-up?"

"The best! I was so fired up from the news that I slayed everything. I am so ready for tonight."

"I'm glad we could inspire you."

"I was feeling really nervous before but not anymore." She sounded out of breath from all the excitement, and she paused for a second. "This is our year, Court."

Josh walked up behind me and kissed my shoulder, and I looked up into his smiling eyes.

"Finally."

CHAPTER EIGHT

"To our Olympians, Courtney and Joshua." Mrs. Cassar raised her glass of champagne. "May you have the time of your life in Sochi!"

All of us at the large table lifted our glasses and clinked them together. We'd taken over the back of the hotel's pub with our late-night celebration. Liza had won gold an hour earlier but was hung up at the arena doing media, so we'd had to hold our party without her. Em, Sergei, and the twins had joined us along with our families and Mrs. Cassar.

Quinn and Alex reached across the table to tap their apple juice to my champagne, and our glasses made a loud chime.

"Are you excited to go to Russia again?" I asked them.

They nodded their blond heads in tandem.

"Our babushka and dedushka are gonna be there," Alex said.

Sergei's parents still lived in Moscow, and they usually only saw Liza and the twins once a year.

"I bet they can't wait to see your cute little faces." I pinched their cheeks.

"Coco," Quinn whined and backed away. "We're not

babies."

"Then how come you still call me Coco?"

They'd started doing it when they were learning to talk and couldn't say my name. I loved it but couldn't resist ribbing them about it.

"Because…" Quinn looked at her brother.

"If you hear Coco you know it's us calling you," Alex finished.

"It's our special nickname for you," Quinn said.

"Aww, well I hope you never stop using it, then."

Josh stretched his arm across the back of my chair. "I'm so glad we're not one of those couples that has cutesy nicknames for each other."

"Like Cupcake and Honey Bun?"

He laughed. "I love how your mind immediately went to dessert-themed names."

"That's because I've been ready for a huge piece of Boston Cream Pie ever since I saw it on the menu."

He leaned in close to me. "I was hoping we could skip dessert."

The intention in his soft voice lit me up inside, and I rubbed his thigh under the table.

"Maybe we can get it to go," I said.

One corner of his mouth curled up, and he tickled the nape of my neck. "Fun with chocolate."

I grinned. "I love how your mind works, too."

"I'd also like to make a toast," Mrs. Tucker announced.

My smile weakened, and I hesitantly picked up my glass, not knowing what to expect from the woman who never handed out well-wishes.

"To Courtney and Josh. May you have greater success in Sochi."

It took all my restraint not to roll my eyes. Her toast was her not-so-subtle way of expressing her displeasure that we hadn't won the title. I'd heard her muttering about it to Josh's dad when we'd arrived at the restaurant.

Everyone raised their glasses and drank, but Mrs. Cassar stared down Mrs. Tucker. "The Olympics are about more than results. These two have waited a lifetime to have this experience together."

"It's a competition, is it not? Results are important," Mrs. Tucker said.

"If they enjoy themselves, the results will come," Mrs. Cassar countered.

I couldn't let the volley across the table continue. This was a celebration fourteen years in the making, and Josh's mom was *not* going to ruin it.

"Josh and I know we can skate better than we did this week, and we plan to do that in Russia. We also plan to have fun every moment we're there."

We hadn't had time to talk about our strategy at the Olympics since we were still in the afterglow of making the team, but I felt confident Josh would agree with me.

He squeezed my shoulder, confirming his agreement. "And we're not going to put any pressure on ourselves."

"What about the team event?" Mrs. Tucker asked. "You won't be able to avoid pressure there."

"We don't even know yet if we'll be picked to be in it," Josh said.

I grabbed my glass and swigged the remainder of my drink. If Mrs. Tucker made one more snarky comment, I wasn't going to be able to keep my mouth shut.

"You'd better be in it," she said. "It's your only chance at a medal."

No more!

"You know what? We've—" I started, but Sergei cut me off.

"There will be plenty of time to address the team event later. Courtney and Josh have worked a very long time for this day, so nothing is going to interrupt this party." He picked up the bottle of champagne and topped off Mrs. Tucker's glass.

"Here, here," Mrs. Cassar said.

I gave Sergei a little smile of thanks for saving me from causing an ugly scene. I shouldn't let anything Josh's mom said irritate me. This was our night, our party, our time to feel nothing but complete ecstasy. We'd achieved our goal, dammit. First place, second place... it didn't matter. We were *in*.

"Sergei, can you give us some Russian lessons before the trip?" Dad asked.

"We can teach you," Quinn said. "We know all the letters and numbers."

She and Alex began reciting the Russian alphabet, and Emily said, "Not so loud. The whole restaurant doesn't need a lesson."

Dad chuckled. "Sounds like we have our tour guides lined up."

"I really wish I was going," Stephanie said. "I bet there will be killer parties every night."

"You're sorrier about missing the parties than not seeing us skate?" Josh asked with a teasing smile.

"That's not what I said. I'd love to see my beautiful creations in action on Olympic ice. And the people wearing them, of course."

The waitress delivered our dinner, and I devoured every last crumb on my plate. My stomach had been so unsettled that I hadn't enjoyed a meal all week. Sergei saved me again by keeping Josh's parents occupied with small talk, so Mrs. Tucker didn't have time to spread her sourness all over us.

Mrs. Cassar insisted we finish off our final bottle of champagne before we left, so Josh and I ate our dessert with the group. Neither of us were big drinkers, so we were both smiling like fools throughout dinner, and Josh's cheeks had turned a rosy color. When the party finally broke up, he and I raced ahead of everyone to the elevators and stumbled inside.

The doors closed, and Josh backed me against the wall, his hands on my hips. He pressed his lips to mine, and I gasped into his mouth. All the blood rushed from my head, giving me a dizzying thrill. I wound my arms around Josh and anchored us together.

He came up for air but kept his firm hold on me. "I've been dying to do that since we got our score."

I dropped one hand between our bodies and hooked my finger through his belt loop. "I've been dying to do a lot of things to you."

He returned his mouth to mine, but the ding of the elevator forced my eyes open. Two young skater girls got on and stared at us with wide eyes, clearly holding in their giggles. Josh and I hastily split apart, also biting our lips so we wouldn't spew laughter everywhere.

The doors opened on our floor, and we laughed all the way down the long hall to our room. I pulled off my ballet flats and danced across the carpet.

"I feel like I'm floating on a cloud, and it's not just from the champagne buzz," I said.

Josh watched me with a huge grin. "Seeing the pure happiness on your face is the best part of all of this."

"It's just as much relief as happiness." I removed the hair band from my ponytail, releasing my long curls. "I think today was the most nervous I've ever been in my life."

"Same here. When Roxanne and Evan's score came up, it hit me all at once and I started freaking out."

"I could see in your eyes that you were freaking out."

His expression turned serious, and he closed the gap between us. "I just… I couldn't be the reason you missed out on the team again. I wouldn't have been able to forgive myself if I'd made a mistake that cost us."

"Josh," I said softly and placed my hands on his chest. Emotion choked me, and I had to swallow hard before I could continue.

"I never would've blamed you. I wouldn't be here if it wasn't for you. I thought the Olympics were never going to happen for me, but then you asked me to skate with you, and you gave me another chance." I slid even closer and hugged his waist. "You gave me my dream."

He gazed at me quietly before cupping his hands under my chin. "And you give me mine. Every moment we're together."

Our lips met, and I could have sworn I really was floating. I stood on the tips of my toes to reach Josh's height, but I lost my balance and took us both down onto the bed. He looked up at me, his blue eyes sharpening with desire, and he pulled me into another fiery kiss that made me gasp again. No one interrupted us that time, and he continued to take my breath away until we collapsed into sleep deep into the night.

I woke up a few hours later nestled in the crook of Josh's arm, one leg stretched across his body. He silenced his phone alarm and brushed my hair from my face.

"Morning, Beautiful," he said.

I smiled and kissed his shoulder. "Mornings don't get much better than this one."

"It was a pretty sweet night, too." His mouth spread into a wicked grin.

I pushed up to see the time on the clock, but another item on the nightstand caught my eye. "Our Daruma! We get to color his other eye now."

I reached over Josh and grabbed the doll and the green marker beside it. Settling back against the pillows, I set the Daruma on Josh's chest and uncapped the marker.

"Ready?" I asked.

We held the figurine together, and Josh covered my hand with his as he'd done on New Year's Eve. Soon we had a pair of colorful eyes that didn't match but that represented the two of us and the highest high of our partnership.

"Daruma selfie?" Josh picked up his phone.

I laughed. "Yes, this moment needs to be captured for sure."

We perched the doll between our faces and smiled as Josh clicked the camera button.

"You're not posting that anywhere, right?" I said.

"No way. I'm the only one who gets to see how gorgeous you look in bed."

He stroked my side, and his hand traveled over my hip and down my thigh, awakening every inch of my body. We had a full schedule of activities that day, but I didn't want this glorious morning to end.

I dragged my fingernails lightly down Josh's hard stomach, and his abs clenched under my touched. "Do we have time for a little more celebrating?"

His answer was a resounding unspoken *Yes*, and we barely made it to exhibition practice at the arena on time. After a partial run-through of our show program and a lot of goofing off with the other medalists, we went upstairs for an event we always enjoyed, the federation's donor breakfast. As soon as we walked into the club room, three of our fans spotted us and jumped out of the buffet line to greet us.

"Congratulations!" they exclaimed.

We'd talked to the women at a number of competitions and shows the past four years as they'd been some of our strongest supporters. We gave all of them hugs and chatted and took photos while a line of more fans formed behind them.

"When do you find out if you're competing in the team event?" Darlene asked.

I thought back to Mrs. Tucker's comments at dinner, and a hint of tension crept into my neck. This was the only thing that could slightly deflate my off-the-charts happiness. Part of the Sochi Pact Liza and I had made was competing in the team event, but losing to Roxanne and Evan had complicated the situation. Josh and I were no longer the clear favorite for the one pairs spot in the competition.

"Probably not until we get to Sochi," Josh said. "The federation has certain criteria it's using to make the decision."

"You guys had a better season overall than Roxanne and Evan. That has to count for something."

"And you're way nicer," Darlene said in a low voice.

We all laughed, and I said, "I'll reserve comment on that."

For the next hour we posed for countless photos and signed program after program. My stomach rumbled as I smelled the plates of bacon and eggs sailing past us, but we had to make sure all the fans received attention before we hit the buffet.

When the crowd around us cleared, Josh and I headed straight for what was left of the food. Just as we reached for plates, our phones dinged simultaneously with text notifications. Our eyes locked with excitement, and we tapped on our screens. The sender of the message was the head of the federation's International Committee.

Congratulations on your Olympic team qualification! Please report to the media room at noon for a press conference.

I stared at the text and read it over and over to myself. *Congratulations on your Olympic team qualification!* That small sentence gave me chills. Even though we'd known yesterday we'd earned our spot and the text was just a formality for us, seeing the words made it all the more real. All the past disappointments, all the heartache... none of it mattered anymore. I would no longer have to live with *What if?* torturing me. My throat tightened, and I blinked hard as tears filled my eyes.

Josh grinned and showed me his phone with the identical message. "Pretty cool, huh?"

I nodded quickly and covered my mouth as I felt a sob about to escape. I rushed out of the room and into the corridor, and the tears sprang forth.

Josh caught up to me and brought me into his arms. I hid my face against his sweater so the people trickling in and out of the breakfast wouldn't see me ugly crying.

"I didn't want to lose it in there with everyone watching," I mumbled.

He kissed the top of my head. "They all know what you've been through, how close you've come in the past. I'm surprised you haven't lost it before now."

"I think I still felt like I was in a fantasy, but seeing it in the official text made the reality of it hit me."

"It's going to get even more official at the press conference. Should I carry some extra tissues for you?" He smiled and touched my cheek.

"I don't know how I'm going to get through it without bawling. Or the exhibition later. Why did I let you talk me into skating to 'The Impossible Dream?' That song makes me cry just listening to it." I laughed between my tears.

"I'm fully expecting to get choked up myself, so at least we'll be an emotional mess together."

I hugged him again and then dabbed at my eyes. "I should just hang a box of Puffs around my neck for the rest of the day."

CHAPTER NINE

THE SKATERS' LOUNGE BACKSTAGE AT THE arena had been filled with tension all week, but now with the competition over, it had become party central. There were a few disappointed medalists who'd narrowly missed making the Olympic team (something with which I could identify all too well), but most of the skaters couldn't stop smiling as they waited to perform in the exhibition.

I had my phone out and was snapping photos with everyone in my path. I spotted my training mates Caitlin and Ernie, who'd won the junior pairs title, and we took what would amount to an entire film roll of funny-face pictures.

"We promise we'll keep Team Cape Cod going strong next year," Ernie said as we hugged.

"Oh, I know you will. I'll be stopping by the rink every chance I get to see you guys."

"Where's Josh?" Caitlin asked. "We need a group pic."

I looked around the crowded room and down the corridor to the ice. "He was here a few minutes ago. I'll grab you when I find him."

I needed to stretch and get mentally ready for our

performance, so I moved away from the party for some alone space. Caitlin and Ernie laughed together as they joined the other junior champions for a photo, and I thought about what Ernie had said.

I'd been so focused on competing that I hadn't had time to dwell on this being my last nationals. It was hard to imagine my life without competitive skating and not working toward this event every year. January had been the focal point of my year for so long. As excited as I was to start college, I couldn't deny feeling a little scared and a lot sad over leaving this crazy world behind.

My stomach tensed, and I paced along the far end of the lounge. I shouldn't have let my brain go there. I was already getting wound up enough about skating. Josh had put so much heart into choreographing our program that he'd created just for this event. I didn't want to get so emotional that I screwed up the elements.

I remembered clearly the day Josh had brought up his idea. We'd just finished our competition in France and were spending the day sightseeing in Paris. We sat in a charming café, drinking coffee and enjoying the best chocolate éclairs we'd ever tasted.

"I've been thinking about nationals and something new we could do for the exhibition," Josh said.

"I thought we would just do our 'Titanium' program since we don't have much time to work on something else," I said.

"I love that program. It's so badass." Josh took a long sip from his cup. "But I have an idea I really want to put together. The song inspired me as soon as I listened to it."

"What song is it?"

He hesitated slightly, and I became more curious.

"'The Impossible Dream.'"

My first reaction was to laugh, and Josh quickly said, "I know what you're thinking."

"That if we don't make the team, there's no way I'm skating to a song about chasing an impossible dream?"

"We're going to make the team, so that won't be an issue."

I rested my chin on my hand. "I'm all about being confident, but this ain't my first rodeo. I have to prepare myself for all scenarios."

"I totally get that. What I need to explain, though, is the reason the song spoke to me. It's not about our Olympic quest." He grasped my other hand. "It's about you."

"Me?"

"For so long, being with you seemed almost impossible, but I never stopped dreaming of you. You were my 'unreachable star' as the song says." He grazed his thumb over my knuckles, and I shivered from his gentle touch. "But I just had this feeling I would have a chance someday. And here we are."

I smiled. "Here we are."

"That's why it would be incredibly special for me to create this program for you and to skate it with you in Boston."

My heart ballooned further, and I angled forward over the tiny table. "Well, how can I say no to that?"

The ice dance champions waltzed past me, their sneakers squeaking on the floor, and I came back to the present. I stretched one arm in front of me and extended one leg behind me to loosen my muscles.

Em walked with purpose toward the locker rooms, not looking my way, and I wondered what was up with her serious expression. She normally wouldn't be backstage at the exhibition, but she and Chris had been honored during intermission with all the country's past Olympic gold medalists. She'd been teary then, but she looked on a mission now.

I trailed behind her and found where Josh had been hiding. Em went up to him and gave him a long hug, and I stayed behind a TV monitor and watched them talk quietly. Josh looked serious, too, and seemed just as nervous as he'd been before our free skate. The butterflies swarming in my stomach multiplied. I *really* wanted to skate this performance lights-out for him.

Em said something, and Josh finally broke into a smile. They hugged again, and I walked over to them, brightening Josh's face even more.

"You disappeared on me," I said.

"Sorry, I just wanted to do one last run-through in my head, and there was too much going on out there."

"Yeah, I tried to escape myself."

"I'm heading back to my seat." Em hugged me hard. "Have a great skate."

She sounded on the verge of crying again. I supposed it was just the emotion of the whole event getting to her. I was in no position to question anyone's tears after I'd sobbed my way through the press conference. I'd struggled to form one coherent sentence.

Josh and I held hands and drifted toward the tunnel. With the stark lights in the arena dimmed and a DJ spinning tunes between each skater, the atmosphere had an entirely different feel from when we'd last been on the ice. We stood next to the boards, shrouded in darkness, and watched the men's bronze medalist skate to Jason Mraz.

Josh moved behind me and played with my curls, his fingertips lightly teasing my bare shoulders. Unlike our competitive programs where I wore my hair up, I could leave it down and let it fly in our show programs. The soft style went perfectly with my pale pink dress.

I turned to face Josh, and I connected with his eyes in the dim light. He looked especially handsome dressed all in black. I was trying to calm myself before getting on the ice, but taking in his hotness only made my heart beat faster.

He pulled me close and clasped his hands on the small of my back. "You were my inspiration for this program, but after yesterday, I know the song must have deep meaning for you, too."

I smiled and squeezed his biceps. "I reached my own unreachable star."

He kissed my forehead, and I took slow breaths in and out. Even though we hadn't run through the program many times, all I had to do was look at Josh and the love between us would take over and guide us through every step. I'd felt it when we'd practiced at home. This program wasn't about the elements. It was about the connection we'd had since we'd met so many years ago.

One of the volunteers signaled to us to get ready, so we inched nearer to the ice door. The DJ cued up some dance music, and I bounced on my guards to stay warm. The closer we got to the ice, the more goosebumps formed on my arms.

The veteran skater coming off the ice high-fived us, and we switched places with him. We stood under the spotlight near the boards and received applause even before our introduction. Once we were introduced and we skated to center ice, the crowd really let loose, giving me added goosebumps. How lucky was I to have had my first and my last nationals in my hometown?

Josh and I separated for our starting pose, and the moment the music began we skated toward each other, joining our hands as we met. We quickened our strokes and sailed across the rink, and right on the first rise of the music, Josh tossed me over his head for a massive triple twist.

We slowed to match the tempo of the piano, and Josh swept his hand over my cheek. His eyes captured mine, and as we glided in the spotlight with blackness all around us, it truly felt as if only the two of us existed.

Through each movement our eyes stayed connected, and the love in Josh's heightened my emotions. We spun into our rotational lift, the one we'd done the first time we'd ever skated together, and a lump formed in my throat. I'd known then that I'd found my skating soul mate. What I hadn't realized but knew with certainty now was Josh was also my life soul mate.

The song rose toward its soaring high, and overwhelming joy rose inside me as we sped across the ice. Josh took hold of my left leg, and he lifted me high into the air, higher than I'd ever been. It was like I was standing on air and flying. I spread my arms wide and couldn't hold in the tears any longer.

Josh brought me down into his arms, and we both shook with emotion as we glided to a stop in a tight embrace. The crowd lit up the darkness with cheers, and I shuddered harder with sobs. Josh held onto me and buried his lips in my hair.

"Better than I ever could've dreamt it," he said.

We left the ice after an endless ovation, and Liza was waiting for us with big hugs. She sniffled in my ear and blotted her eyes with a tissue.

"I'll have to fix my makeup before I skate. Thanks for making us all cry." She punched my arm.

I laughed. "You're welcome. You're going to have people in tears, too."

Her "Beneath Your Beautiful" program that Josh had choreographed always choked me up, especially because I knew the deep meaning it had to her.

She fiddled with her long, sleek ponytail. "I think everyone here is in a state of either laughing hysterically or bawling uncontrollably. This has been the craziest day."

"And there's more to come," Josh said.

Liza ran off to do a mirror check before her performance, and Josh and I went to the locker rooms to change into our free skate costumes. We had to sit for team photos on the ice after the show. When Liza's name was called, we ran up the tunnel and parked ourselves rinkside for a front-row view. Her heartfelt performance did make me misty-eyed, and I hurried afterward to collect myself for the finale of the show.

The Olympic team members filled the ice, and as the DJ played The Black Eyed Peas, we tossed autographed Frisbees and T-shirts into the screaming audience. Between throwing goodies, we took turns carrying an American flag around the rink and soaking in the energy of the fans. After being on the outside looking in at all the Olympic hoopla in the past, I flew across the ice and waved the flag high and proud, so honored to finally be in the exclusive club.

When we had to say our goodbyes, everyone retreated to the lounge to wait for the okay to return to the ice, but I stayed at the edge of the tunnel, watching the crowd disappear. The last bodies emptied the seats, and I quickly hopped back onto the ice. As I did a few twizzles, I heard another set of blades whooshing behind me. I looked over my shoulder and smiled at the sight of Josh.

"No surprise we're the most eager to get out here," I said.

He stopped in front of me and took both my hands. "No one else is coming."

I tilted my head in confusion, and I became more surprised when music began to play on the sound system. I recognized the haunting cello notes right away.

"Your Hands Are Cold" from *Pride and Prejudice.* One of our most special songs.

My heart began to race.

Could it be... ?

"What..." I squeaked. "Why is this song..."

"Because it was playing the first time I kissed you, and it was our first program as a team. And we're here on the ice because that's where I first saw you. A moment that changed my life." He wet his lips, and I held my breath, waiting for him to continue. "And I hope today will be another first for us. The first day of our future together."

I had to breathe, and it came out as a small cry. Josh bent on one knee, and our hands trembled together. He gazed up at me, his clear blue eyes so bright and alive, and I bit my lip to stop from screaming "Yes!" before he even asked the question.

"Court, you have inspired me and challenged me and made me a stronger, better man." His voice broke, and my own throat tightened. "You are my first and my forever love."

He fumbled inside his pocket, and the tears brimming in my eyes escaped onto my cheeks. Opening the black velvet box, he revealed a dazzling diamond ring. I let out a louder cry and immediately started nodding. I couldn't help myself.

Josh gave me a brilliant smile. "Courtney Elizabeth Carlton, will you marry me?"

"Yes, yes, yes!"

He shot to his feet and wrapped me in his arms, lifting me from the ice. I'd had so many memorable moments on the ice in my career, but none more incredible than this one. Nothing could top this. *Ever.*

Applause and catcalls echoed in the empty building, and I turned to see all the skaters watching from the kiss and cry. Liza stood at the front, doing a happy dance.

"And I thought this week couldn't get any better," I said.

"Ready to make it official?" Josh took the ring from the box.

"I've never been more ready for anything in my life."

He kissed the back of my hand and slipped the diamond onto my finger. The round cut and the plain platinum band were classic and timeless. The perfect symbol of our love for each other.

I looked into his eyes and whispered through my tears, "I love you so much, Joshua Joseph Tucker."

We melted into a kiss, and more cheers rang out. Two familiar little voices carried above the noise, and I saw the twins, Em, Sergei, and our families walking down to the boards.

I gaped at Josh. "Everyone knew?"

"I needed Em's help setting it all up, and I talked to your parents after I bought the ring."

"When I saw you with Em before we skated, I thought you were nervous about the program."

"I was excited about skating but nervous as hell about

this." He smiled shyly.

"You had to know I would say yes."

"I had a good feeling." He grinned. "But I just wanted everything to be perfect."

"It was. It is." I framed his face with my hands. "It always will be with you."

We kissed again but were interrupted by Quinn chanting, "Coco and Josh! Coco and Josh!"

We laughed and skated over to the group, where we were bombarded with hugs. I steered clear of Josh's parents, wanting to avoid any awkward attempts, or more likely, non-attempts at affection.

"No long engagement," Mrs. Cassar said. "I'm not getting any younger."

I hooked my arm around Josh's waist. "I'm more than okay with that rule."

"You could get married in Sochi," Mrs. Tucker said. "The media would fall in love with that story."

I lifted my eyebrows. "I didn't mean *that* soon."

"We're not making our wedding a spectacle," Josh said.

"But think of the financial opportunity it would be."

"Mom." Josh just shook his head.

"Let's see the ring," Stephanie said.

I extended my hand, and Quinn gasped. "It's so pretty!"

"Very nice job, Joshua," Mrs. Cassar said.

Mrs. Tucker leaned in for a closer look. "How cute."

Josh's body grew tense, and my face warmed, but I wasn't embarrassed over the size of the diamond. I was embarrassed for Josh, who had to claim this woman as his mother.

"It's gorgeous," Em said in a harsher, louder voice than usually came from her.

The photographer called to us for the photo shoot backstage, so we had to cut our celebration short. We'd have more time to party at the Olympic team reception in a couple of hours. Or in Mrs. Tucker's case, more time to be a nuisance.

Between now and then, she'll probably draw up a pre-nup agreement.

Josh laced his fingers through mine as we skated to the door. "Are you sure you're okay with being tied to my mom for life?"

"As long as she stays on her side of the country most of the time, I can totally handle her." I shifted to face Josh. "But I wouldn't care if you came with a family of vampires. Nothing and no one would make me question marrying you."

He eased into a wide smile and bent his head, touching his lips to my neck. His teeth nipped at my skin, and I laughed and swatted his chest.

We were engaged and going to the Olympics.

What is this life?!

CHAPTER TEN

I PAINTED MY LIPS WITH A shimmering coat of gloss and stood back to examine myself in the bathroom mirror. After the nonstop day I'd had — from the donor breakfast to the press conference to an autograph signing and then the exhibition — I should look exhausted, but my eyes were wide and shining. I was more than ready for the team reception. Not only was I being honored for the biggest achievement of my life, but I was going to walk into the room as Josh's fiancée.

Cue the internal squealing.

I'd been doing a lot of that the past hour.

I put my hand over my heart, and the ring sparkled against my red dress. I couldn't stop looking at it. It was like I was afraid it might disappear.

It's not going anywhere. You're going to be wearing this the rest of your life.

That thought warmed me through and through. My reflection smiled as brightly as the diamond shined, and I opened the door to see the man who'd made me so deliriously happy.

Josh stood at the window, looking out at the lights of

Boston. He'd continued his all-black look from earlier with a dark suit, shirt, and tie, and he looked *beyond* incredible. His eyes made a slow sweep over me, and the warmth inside me bloomed into searing heat.

"You are a goddess." He took a few steps toward me. "I can't believe I get to marry you."

I walked over to him and smoothed my hands down his lapels. "And you are the sweetest and the sexiest man alive."

He curled his hand around the back of my neck and gave me a passionate kiss, and I clung to his jacket. I'd have to redo my lip gloss, but I'd happily apply it a hundred times over for more kisses like that.

He linked our hands, and he ran his thumb over the band of my ring. "I love seeing this on your finger."

"How long have you had it?"

"Since right before Christmas. It was so hard waiting to give it to you, but I really wanted to do it here."

"What would've happened if we hadn't made the team? As confident as you were, I know you must've had a backup plan."

He smiled. "I didn't let myself think too much about the backup plan, but it would've been a trip to the beach house in Malibu."

We'd gone to his family's beach house a few times since our first visit after the 2010 Olympics. On that trip, Josh had asked me to skate with him shortly after we'd arrived, and we'd had an unforgettable night afterward.

"A place where we had a very important first together," I said and leaned into him until our lips just barely touched.

"Best day of my life until today," he said.

We did more delicious damage to my lip gloss, and then we just stood quietly, our heads bent together. These were the first silent moments we'd had with each other since Josh had proposed. I knew it was silly to think that one little question could change things, but I felt a different energy between us.

As strong as our love had always been, something even more powerful hummed between us.

"You know, I was getting kinda worried that you weren't thinking about marriage anymore since you'd stopped talking about it," I said. "Did you do that on purpose?"

"I didn't want to give away any hints of what I was planning." He hugged my waist. "So, you were really worried?"

"Yes! And you kept faking me out with all those gifts. You can't be all mysterious and tell a girl she has to stay up until midnight on New Year's Eve unless you have a ring to surprise her with."

"You didn't like the Daruma?"

"I love the little guy, but he can't compare to this." I grinned and held up my left hand.

He pointed to the nightstand. "You're hurting his feelings. Good thing he's already helped us reach our goal."

I laughed, but as memories of New Year's Eve filtered through my mind, I remembered something that made me stop. My skin prickled with anxiousness, and I stared at Josh.

"We haven't reached our goal yet."

Josh's forehead wrinkled. "Aren't we on our way to the Olympic team dinner?"

"When we colored in the first eye, we said our goal was to skate together at the Olympics."

"And we earned the right to do that yesterday."

"But we haven't actually skated there yet, and we went ahead and painted the second eye. We were supposed to wait until we achieved our goal." My voice lifted higher as my breathing accelerated.

"It's just semantics, Babe."

I shook my head. "Good luck charms aren't something to mess with. What if we jacked up our karma?"

Josh placed his hands on both sides of my face and tilted my chin to look at him. "Nowhere in the Daruma story does it say everything must be taken literally. There's no bad karma coming our way. I promise."

I eyed the doll and took a few deep breaths. Why was I getting so worked up about this? I couldn't let paranoia and superstition drive me batty. Just because life was amazingly wonderful right now didn't mean something bad was due to happen.

"I think I'm just going to be scared until we're actually standing on the ice in Sochi. I've waited so long for this that I can't help worrying."

His thumbs softly stroked my face. "I totally understand. Just remember that doll has no power over anything."

"Now who's hurting his feelings?"

He laughed and held me to his chest, and I snuck one more look at our blue-and-green-eyed friend. Later when Josh fell asleep, I was going to apologize to the Daruma.

Just in case.

"THIS PLACE IS A skating groupie's dream right now," Stephanie said as she craned her neck to scan the hotel bar.

I laughed and sipped my diet soda. Everyone from the reception had descended upon the bar after the party ended, and it had already been packed with former Olympians, legendary coaches, and anyone and everyone important in the sport. Josh, Stephanie, and I had been lucky to snag a small table in the middle of the action.

"Thank God your parents have an early flight and didn't follow us here," I said.

"I'm surprised my mom isn't here anyway. She was working the room at the reception," Josh said. "I'm glad she wasn't all over us for once, but I don't even want to know what she was up to."

Stephanie took a long drink of her red wine. "She's on a

mission about the team event. She was probably trying get the scoop on what the fed's plan is."

"Fabulous," I muttered. "Last thing we need is our misguided cheerleader politicking for us."

"Let's talk about something more pleasant, like your wedding." Stephanie emptied her glass and signaled to the waitress for another. She'd been throwing back wine all night, and I'd learned that tipsy Stephanie was actually a lot of fun.

"Marriage isn't for me," she continued. "I'd rather keep my men on rotation."

Josh just shook his head, and I snickered behind my napkin. Stephanie went on, "But you two are one of those disgustingly perfect couples meant to be married."

"I'm disgusted by our perfection on a daily basis," Josh said, managing to hold a straight face.

I laughed and rubbed my arms as freezing air seeped through the lobby into the open bar. Josh took off his suit jacket and draped it over my shoulders.

"See?" Stephanie waved her hands at us. "So sweet it's revolting."

"I think you should definitely do the toast at our wedding. This is some great material," I said, still laughing.

"When is this big event happening? I need to put it on my busy calendar," she said.

"We've been engaged all of four hours."

"Come on, I *know* you've been thinking about it longer than that. Admit it. You have your whole dream wedding planned."

"I... I don't..." I sputtered as Josh just grinned at me. "I mean, maybe I've had a few thoughts..."

"I knew it." Stephanie slapped the table. "So, spill it."

"I don't know... I guess I've always pictured something on the beach."

"Very Cape Cod." She nodded but suddenly stopped. "Ohh, I could make you an amazing beachy dress. Something soft and gauzy and romantic."

My eyebrows popped up. "You're offering to make my wedding dress?"

"Well, I have to make sure my brother has a fashionable bride on his arm."

Josh turned to me. "I like your idea a lot."

"Really?" I hadn't envisioned every detail of my future wedding like many girls did, but the setting had been the one constant in my daydreams of Josh and me saying our vows.

"As soon as you said beach, I could imagine it. I can see you in that dress, the ocean breeze in your hair..." He tucked a long curl behind my ear.

"You're killing me," Stephanie said.

I reluctantly tore my eyes from Josh's warm gaze and smiled at Stephanie. "You started it, bringing up the wedding."

"I can't believe you're getting married, Josh. To me, you'll always be the boy who played Barbie with me."

Josh covered his face with one hand, and I leaned forward onto the table. "I must hear more about this."

"Josh used to—"

"I'll explain," Josh jumped in. "Let me make it clear that I was always Ken, but her Barbie and my Ken were brother and sister. Never a couple," he said emphatically. "And I did manly things like fix the Corvette."

"I had like ten of each doll, so I used another Ken for my boyfriend," Stephanie said. "There was Malibu Ken and Doctor Ken and—"

"I bet you had the dream house, didn't you?" I said.

"Of course."

I sighed. "I always wanted the dream house."

"Want me to get you one for a wedding present?" Josh asked.

I giggled. "Only if you promise to play with me."

He gave me a sly smile, and Stephanie groaned. "If you're

going from sweet to kinky now, I really need more wine."

"Tell me more about young Josh," I said. "I want all the embarrassing stories he's never told me."

"Hmm... fetus Josh stories..." She tapped her fingers together. "Oh! He was terrified of clowns, and once we were at a birthday party for a kid from the rink, and there was *a car full of clowns*. It was like a damn circus. Josh took off running down the street and had to be chased down."

"Clowns are evil," he said. "Haven't you seen the movie *It*?"

"They are pretty creepy," I said. "I would've paid to see your mom chase you down the street, though."

Stephanie let out a loud peal of laughter. "As if she was there. Our nanny Teresa took us to the party."

"I learned a bunch of Spanish curse words that day." Josh chuckled.

Stephanie drank from her fresh glass the waitress had just delivered, and she clapped her hands. "I have another story. Josh had an imaginary friend named Bob. He used to go everywhere with us — the rink, piano lessons, the beach. Mom would get so annoyed when she'd hear Josh talking to him."

His cheeks tinted pink, and I touched his leg. "Lots of kids have imaginary friends."

"How come I don't remember Dad ever giving you a hard time about it?" Stephanie asked.

"He didn't know. Unless Mom told him."

"You never talked to Bob in front of Dad?" Stephanie asked.

"That was kinda the point of Bob." Josh looked down at his soda. "He was there when Dad wasn't."

Silence fell over the table, and the laughter and chatter around us seemed to fade far into the background. Josh picked at his napkin, tearing off jagged pieces.

"God, that's so depressing," Stephanie said.

My chest ached as I pictured tiny Josh... sweet, shy little

Josh... so desperate for a relationship with his dad that he made up an imaginary father who would always be around. Already high on emotion from the crazy day, I felt myself about to burst into tears. I had to get out of there before I made a scene.

"I need to go to the ladies' room." I shed Josh's jacket and high-tailed it away from the table.

I had to fight my way through the crowd, and I was almost to the edge of the bar when a hand shot out and grabbed my arm. I swung my head around and saw Roxanne sitting at a high-top table.

"Excuse me." I pulled out of her grasp.

"Can you tell your future mother-in-law that money can't buy you a spot in the team event?" Her twangy voice slurred as she spoke.

My urge to cry had died, and now only annoyance bubbled in my chest. "What are you talking about?"

"I saw her running her mouth at the party. What's she trying to do? Bribe the fed to get you in?"

"No one is bribing anyone. I think you'd better cut yourself off." I pointed to her half-empty glass.

"You guys will do anything to be the darlings of the federation, won't you? How long did you have the proposal planned?"

"That wasn't a publicity stunt."

"*Right.* I was shocked you didn't do it when the cameras were rolling, but your home video is all over the internet already, so congratulations." She did a slow clap.

I stared at her, stuck for words. Sergei had recorded us on his phone so we'd have the moment captured forever, but he would never have posted it online.

Mrs. Tucker. She must have asked him to send it to her.

I folded my arms over my chest. "Josh and I didn't post the video."

"It doesn't matter who in your little circle did it. All the publicity in the world isn't getting you our spot in the event."

"They don't need publicity," Stephanie said as she came to my side. "They're the better team."

"*We* are the champions." Roxanne grew louder. "They got lucky that other teams screwed up or Courtney here would've been a loser for the third time."

Stephanie reached out and knocked over Roxanne's glass, spilling white wine all over her gold dress. Roxanne gasped, while my mouth fell open with no sound. The people standing around us watched with wide eyes.

Roxanne jumped up, stumbling on her platform heels, and got in Stephanie's face. "You bitch!"

"And proud of it." Stephanie smirked.

I took hold of her waist and pulled her away from Roxanne. "I think it's time to go."

I hustled her back to our table, where Josh gave us a curious look. "What did I miss?"

My roller coaster of emotions took a sharp curve into amusement, and I dissolved into laughter. "Your sister almost started a rumble with Roxanne."

"No, she started it." Stephanie dropped into her chair. "I was shutting her up."

I gave her a big smile. "You stood up for me."

She rolled her eyes. "Don't get all sappy on me. I've always hated that girl and have been waiting to do something like that."

I nodded slowly, but I knew there was more behind her actions. A few years ago, I wouldn't have believed Stephanie would ever come to my defense, but the weekend had been full of surprises. It was only fitting that it ended with the most bizarre one of all.

CHAPTER ELEVEN

WITH THE VOLUME ON JOSH'S CAR stereo cranked up, he and I sang along to The Temper Trap as we made the familiar drive to the restaurant for work. Our awful attempts at singing falsetto sent us into a fit of laughter, and I didn't realize my phone was ringing until I noticed it lighting up my purse. Liza's photo filled the screen.

"Hey, Cap," I shouted and turned down the stereo volume.

I'd started addressing Liza as such since she'd been named the captain of our Olympic figure skating squad. She was taking her role very seriously, texting all of us daily inspirational quotes and clips from famous sports movies. We weren't leaving for Sochi for ten more days, but I was already so pumped.

"Are you at the party?" Liza asked.

"What party?"

She didn't answer, and I looked at the screen to see if the call had dropped.

"Oh… umm…" she sputtered. "It sounded like you were at a party with the loud music."

"I'm in Josh's car. We're just jamming on our way to work."

She paused again, adding to the weird vibe she was giving me. "Maybe you should put me on speaker," she said. "I have some news."

My smile faded. She didn't exactly sound excited to deliver the news. I tapped the speaker icon and propped my elbow on the armrest.

"What's up?"

"Roxanne and Evan were given the team event spot, and they chose to do both the short and the long. They could've just done one and let you guys do the other, but that would be too unselfish for them."

I rested my head against the seat as I lost some of the excited energy I'd had all week. "That really blows."

"You had a better Grand Prix season *and* finished higher at Worlds last year," Liza said. "But all the federation cares about is the stupid quad Roxanne did at nationals. What are the odds they'll land it again in Sochi?"

"How could the fed not even give us a chance to do the short program? After how well we've skated the past few years?" I said.

"The rules say it's the skaters' choice to do one or both," Liza said.

"But they could step in," Josh piped up. "They do it with everything else."

"It's total BS," Liza said. "You deserve a shot at a medal."

My grip on the phone tightened. Once we'd gotten over the big hurdle of winning an Olympic spot, I'd let the possibility of competing for a team event medal creep into my dreams. What had I been thinking? I'd already been blessed with so much good fortune lately. No way should I have expected more.

"I think they're making a huge mistake," Liza said. "I'd feel more confident with you guys skating. You've been more consistent than Roxanne and Evan all season. They just happened to have the competition of their lives last week."

"Are you doing both the short and the long?" Josh asked.

"Yeah, the fed would kill me if I don't."

"You *are* the best weapon we have," I said. "No pressure."

"What's a little more pressure when I'm already drowning in it?"

Josh and I exchanged concerned glances over the anxiety in her voice. I started to speak, but Liza interrupted, "I'll let you go. I didn't want to be the bearer of bad news, but I didn't want you hearing it from someone like Roxanne."

"I'm glad you called. Thanks for giving us a heads-up," I said. "Try to take it easy, okay?"

"I will. Just ten more days and we'll be in the Village, where we can block out everyone on the outside."

She quickly said goodbye, and I dropped the phone into my purse.

"She's really feeling it now," Josh said.

"Trying to be America's next golden girl... that's a daunting task."

Josh pulled into the restaurant's parking lot and slowed to search for a spot. "Why are there so many cars here so early?"

I spotted a few vehicles with Lighthouse Skating Club decals, and Liza's initial question suddenly made sense.

"It must be a surprise party for us," I said.

Josh turned into an empty space and switched off the engine. "That explains why Mrs. Cassar was acting weird when I saw her this morning."

I opened the mirror on the visor to check my appearance since a roomful of people was soon going to be staring at me.

"Let's not mention Liza's call to anyone. It'll just put a damper on things."

"I'm getting more pissed the more I think about it," Josh

said. "If we'd been picked, we would've shared the spot."

I removed the band from my work-required ponytail and fluffed my hair over my shoulders. "On the bright side, we won't be getting any more hate tweets from Roxanne's minions, accusing us of trying to bribe our way in."

Josh groaned. "My mom is going to blow up my phone when she finds out."

"You might want to change your number."

We climbed out of the car, and I zipped my jacket, blocking out the damp evening chill. Josh took my hand, but I pulled up short before we reached the door.

"I'm wearing my uniform." I frowned. "So much for cute party pics."

"Hey, I fell in love with you in that uniform."

"Was it the necktie or the starchy white shirt that sealed the deal?"

He treated me to a charming sidelong smile. "You wear that shirt and tie like a boss."

I laughed, and Josh swung open the door, triggering a chorus of "Surprise!" from everyone inside. A huge *Congratulations, Courtney and Josh* banner hung above the bar, surrounded by red, white, and blue balloons and white paper bells. They'd covered both our milestones with the decorations.

Josh and I were swallowed up by the crowd, which was an eclectic mix of skaters, coaches, and restaurant regulars. Em grabbed me first and led me behind the bar.

"I brought an outfit from home for you if you want to change," she said.

I started unknotting my tie. "You're the best."

I ducked into the restroom and did a quick change into the dress and boots Em had packed for me. When I rejoined the party, I was immediately tackled by Chris.

"Congrats, Kid."

"Are you still going to call me Kid even after I'm

married?"

"Yes, I am."

His wife, Em's best friend Aubrey, gave me a one-arm hug as she held their eight-month-old daughter on her hip.

"Hi, Noelle." I smoothed my hand over the baby's soft little head. She had her dad's dark wavy hair and her mom's stunning green eyes.

"She loves watching you and Josh skate," Aubrey said. "She was perfectly still the entire time you were on the ice in Boston."

"Aww, that's so cute."

"I've tried showing her videos of me and Em, and she couldn't care less." Chris laughed. "So, you should feel honored."

A couple of singles coaches from the rink crashed our circle, and they started a parade of well-wishes. Many of the restaurant regulars who didn't follow skating asked if Josh and I were going to win a medal in Sochi. I had to explain that we weren't one of the favorites, but we were shooting for a top six finish. What I didn't say was we would've indeed had a strong shot at a medal if we'd been picked for the team event. My anger began to boil again as I was reminded of Liza's news.

Em tapped me on the shoulder, and I put on an extra big smile to hide my disappointment.

"Can you grab Josh so I can get some pics of you with the cake?" she asked.

"Sure. I'll go find him."

I worked my way around the perimeter of the bar and came up empty. Aubrey saw me standing on my toes, trying to see over heads, and she asked, "Looking for someone?"

"My fiancée." I loved saying that.

"He's over by the piano with Chris."

I peeked through an opening in the crowd, and I had no trouble smiling sincerely at the sight before me. I could even feel my heart smiling. Josh was holding Noelle in his arms, and she giggled with delight as he tickled her belly.

"My ovaries just exploded," I said.

"Wait until you go through labor," Aubrey said. "It feels like they really do."

I laughed and slipped between a few adult skaters to get to the piano. Josh grinned at me, and I fingered the hem of Noelle's blue velvet dress.

"I see I've lost you to another girl," I said.

"She's pretty cute, and she doesn't spazz out when I tickle her like someone else does."

I laughed harder, and Chris said, "I asked Josh to hold her while I finish my sandwich. I couldn't bring her back to her mom with roast beef on her dress."

He shoved the last bite into his mouth and took Noelle from Josh so we could meet Em at the dessert table. The large white cake was trimmed with red and blue swirly hearts, and it was topped with the Olympic rings and a fondant American flag. Once again I loved how our engagement and our Olympic berth were celebrated together.

Em made us pose behind the cake with my left hand strategically placed on Josh's arm, and I joked, "This feels like a cross between a prom photo and a wedding portrait."

As soon as Em put down her camera, the twins rushed the table, begging for cake slices heavy on frosting. I barely had a piece in hand before I got swept away from Josh by two of my long-time Saturday night bar patrons.

"Are you and Josh going to win gold like Emily and Chris did?" I was asked.

Jeez, not this question again.

I launched into my explanation of how our career was different from Em and Chris's, but a loud cry of pain from the bar stopped me mid-sentence. I looked over, and my stomach dropped to my toes when I saw Josh holding his hand and grimacing.

The Daruma popped into my head, and all the fears I'd had about bad luck bombarded me. Visions of Josh's hand being sliced open or broken flew through my mind. I hurried toward him, terrified of what I was going to see.

"What happened?"

"Quinn stabbed me with a fork," he said through gritted teeth.

"What?"

Quinn sat behind him on a barstool, and tears poured down her cheeks. "I didn't mean to. Alex pushed me."

"No, I didn't," Alex cried.

I took Josh's elbow. "Let me see your hand."

He uncovered it, revealing four punctures marks near his wrist. Small drops of blood seeped from the wounds. I exhaled deeply as all the terrible injury possibilities evaporated from my mind. This could be fixed with a Band-Aid.

"There's a first aid kit in the kitchen," I said.

Sergei broke through the gawkers around us and gave the twins a stern look. "Come here now. Both of you."

"I'm sorry, Josh," Quinn wailed as she slid off her stool.

Sergei ushered them away from us, and I swiped a napkin from the bar to put pressure on Josh's hand.

"How in the world did she stab you?"

"I was talking to Em's dad and had my hand on the bar, and the next thing I knew Quinn was bumping into me and the fork was in my hand."

"Good Lord. You'd think a seven-year-old could be trusted with real silverware." I shook my head. "Let's go bandage you up."

It took us ten minutes to get to the kitchen because everyone in our path had to see the damage Quinn had done and make jokes about it. While Josh washed his hand in the big industrial sink, I opened the kit and picked out a medium-sized bandage.

"You don't wanna know the thoughts that went through

my head when I saw you in pain," I said.

"Sorry I scared you. It just hurt like hell."

"I can imagine. Who knew we had to watch out for runaway utensils?" I tore open a packet of antibiotic ointment and squeezed it onto the tiny holes in Josh's skin. "I swear, these next ten days can't go by fast enough."

"Are you still thinking about the Daruma?"

I kept my head down and mumbled, "Maybe."

"Would it help if I carried around a four-leaf clover and a rabbit's foot until we get to Russia?"

I glanced up at his teasing smile and couldn't help but crack one myself. "Throw in a horseshoe and we're in business."

FRESH FROM A LONG, hot shower, I stole a T-shirt from Josh's dresser and sat on the bed to comb the tangles from my wet hair. Josh had gone to the main house to borrow bandages from Mrs. Cassar, but he'd been gone longer than such a trip should take.

My stomach rumbled, and I realized I'd done way more talking than eating at the restaurant. I went into the kitchen and poured a bowl of cereal and almond milk, and I carried it back to the bedroom. Sitting cross-legged on the bed, I clicked on my phone and scrolled through the party photos Em had posted online. Lots of heart-eyed emojis were included in the comments from our fans.

The front door opened, and Josh walked through the living room/kitchen, stopping in the bedroom doorway.

"That took a while," I said.

"Mrs. Cassar was still wound up from the party."

"I'm surprised you were able to escape."

I took in a big helping of cereal, and Josh leaned against the door frame, watching me with a little smile. I chewed slowly and smiled back.

"What's that look for?"

"I was just thinking that soon I'll get to see you like this every night."

"Stuffing my face with cereal at midnight?"

He came over and sat beside me on the bed. "It's a very hot look for you."

"I'll have to remember that for future seduction purposes. Candles... lingerie... and cereal."

We laughed together, and Josh scooted closer. "Can I have some?"

I fed him a large spoonful, and he hopped off the bed and tugged his sweater over his head. As I watched him rummage through his dresser, my phone dinged. I took one last lingering look at his ridiculously fit body and opened the text.

Em: *Quinn drew a picture for Josh before she went to sleep.*

The phone dinged again, and a photo popped up. I enlarged it and turned the screen toward Josh. "Quinn made this for you."

On the blue paper she had drawn a curly-haired stick figure wearing a sad face. Below it was neatly written — *Josh, I'm so sorry I hurt you. Love, your friend Quinn.*

Josh smiled. "I'll have to go over there tomorrow and assure her I'm okay."

I typed a quick response to Em and scooped the last few flakes in my bowl. "I didn't think an edible American flag could cause so much drama."

"That's what they were fighting over?" He laughed as he stepped out of his jeans and pulled on a pair of gray sweatpants.

"They usually share so nicely. I'd love our kids to get along as well as they do."

"Our kids." Josh wore the same little smile he'd had earlier, and I found myself mirroring him.

"Speaking of, you looked like a natural with Noelle," I

said.

He stretched out next to me on the bed. "I must've learned it from all the family sitcoms I watched growing up."

I recalled the conversation we'd had with Stephanie at nationals about their childhood. Being so busy with Olympic preparations since then, I hadn't brought up the subject, but I'd wanted to talk to Josh about it.

"Your dad wasn't much of a role model," I said, setting my bowl on the nightstand.

"He was a role model for how not to raise a kid."

I chewed on my lip, unsure if I should ask Josh the question that had been on my mind. "Would you tell me about Bob?"

His head dipped, and he rubbed the back of his neck. "I wish Steph hadn't mentioned that."

"You don't have to be embarrassed. You haven't heard half the goofy stuff I did when I was young."

"I just don't want you to think that I needed major therapy."

"I don't think that." I caressed his arm. "We all have our issues."

He was quiet for a minute. "I don't remember exactly when I made up Bob, but it was when we were at the beach house during the summer. I was maybe five or six."

"You said your dad wasn't there much because he was always working."

"Yeah, it was just me, my mom, and Steph. And Teresa when my mom went out shopping or to play tennis or whatever. Steph didn't like the sand, so she'd never leave the blanket, but I was all about building sand castles." He picked at the bandage on his hand. "I just remember telling Bob my ideas and him helping me."

A slow burn crept into my throat, and I swallowed hard. The image of Josh as a lonely little boy was too much for my heart to handle.

"I guess I got so used to talking to him that I started doing it other places, too. I'd pretend he was there when I skated and when I practiced piano. It makes sense now because my dad hardly ever came to the rink or to my recitals."

I wanted to say something, but the damn tears were choking me. I reached up to blot the corners of my eyes, and Josh lifted his head and caught me.

"Please don't cry." He touched my cheek. "This is another reason I didn't want to tell you about it."

"I'm sorry. It just makes me so angry and so sad that you didn't have the love from your parents that you deserved." I caught my breath and gazed into his beautiful soul. "How could anyone not adore you?"

He didn't speak, but his glistening eyes said it all. He sat up and pulled me into his arms. His hands stroked my back and my hair, but I sensed he needed the comfort as much as I did. I pressed my mouth to his shoulder and kissed his warm skin, and I slowly raised my head to look at him.

"I wish you'd had my parents," I said. "I mean, not my exact parents because then we'd be brother and sister, and that would not be cool."

We both relaxed into laughter, lightening the mood, and I said, "Parents *like* mine is what I meant to say."

Josh curled a lock of my hair around his finger. "All those years I crushed on you, one of the things I noticed about you was how happy you looked with your family. It was one of the many things that drew me to you."

God, it was so unfair. His parents more than had the means to give him their time and attention, but they preferred to substitute material things for emotional sustenance. I hadn't gotten everything I wanted growing up, but I always had the security of my parents' love.

"The way my mom and dad were there for me... that's going to be us. You, me, and our kids." I placed my hand over his heart. "I promise you will never, ever feel alone again. You have me. *All* of me." I leaned in and brushed my lips against his. "Forever."

CHAPTER TWELVE

I STEPPED OUT ONTO THE BALCONY of the dorm room and took
in the sun-splashed splendor of the Olympic Village below.
Our dormitories bordered the calm waters of the Black Sea,
and palm trees dotted the landscape, accentuating the
Village's tropical feel. The temperature was that of a perfect
spring day, so I was proudly wearing one of my new Sochi
2014 T-shirts I'd gotten during team processing at our layover
in Munich. We'd received enough swag to fill two suitcases,
and Liza and I had already managed to spread our new
wardrobe all over our large room.

The Opening Ceremony was a couple of days away, so
we had plenty of time to practice and get acclimated to our
surroundings before we competed. The pairs short program
for the team event was being held the night before the
Opening Ceremony, but thanks to Roxanne, Josh and I didn't
have to prepare for that.

I heard a knock on the door, and I greeted Em with a
smile. She was also dressed head to toe in Olympic gear.

"Where's Liza?" she asked.

"She went down to the dining hall. I'm waiting for Josh to

wake up from his nap."

Em's phone trilled, and she read the screen. "Aunt Deb's texting me pics of the kids doing their schoolwork. They keep asking why they have to stay in a hotel and can't be here with Sergei and me."

"Damn Olympic Committee and all their rules."

"I think it's probably better they're not here because we could never take care of them and also give you, Josh and Liza our full attention."

I led Em onto the balcony and watched a group of Dutch athletes zoom past the building on their orange bikes. I'd met some of them earlier after Josh and I had played pool with a mix of Swedish and Finnish hockey players. Over the course of my career I'd competed at more international events than I could remember, but I'd never been in a melting pot of nations this big.

"I've been so excited about just being here that I hadn't thought much about the actual competition, but when we were at practice this morning and I saw all the media, it dawned on me how many millions of people will be watching. It's *so* many more than I've ever had watching me skate."

"Don't think about that. I've been there and done that at my first Olympics. At the absolute worst moment, in fact." Em laughed and then turned serious. "What you have to do is realize the ice here is the same as it is at home, and everything outside the boards is of no consequence. Not the people in the stands, not the hoopla on the streets, and not the people around the world watching on TV."

"I wish we could've had the team event to get our feet wet. The other top pairs will be able to get those initial Olympic-ice jitters out of the way."

"I want you to know that Sergei and I fought really hard for you and Josh. We went back and forth with the fed and did everything we could to plead your case."

"I know you always have our backs."

"I just wanted to make sure. After what happened four years ago, I don't want you to ever question our commitment as your coaches."

"Em, I told you I completely understood the decision you and Sergei made back then. And how could I not love you for it now? You changed my whole life by bringing Josh to the Cape."

She leaned back against the balcony railing and pulled a few flyaway hairs from her face. "There's something I've never told you about that decision. After Sergei and I met with Stephanie and Josh, I had my phone in my hand, ready to tell them we couldn't coach them. Josh's number was punched in and all I had to do was press dial, but Sergei stopped me. He convinced me we needed to think more about it."

"You were really that close to saying no?"

"Another few seconds and Josh would've never stepped foot on the Cape."

A shudder rolled through me as I considered the awful possibility. "That is a truly terrifying thought."

"It's crazy how one moment in time can completely change the course of people's lives."

"If you'd made that call, Josh would probably be in law school at UCLA right now. I'd like to believe he would've found a way to finally reach out to me even if we hadn't been training together, but who knows what would've happened?"

"He might still be watching YouTube videos of you and dating you in his fantasies." Em smiled.

I laughed. "Thankfully, we'll never have to know."

"I couldn't let you keep giving me credit for bringing Josh into your life when Sergei is really the one responsible. He saved the day."

"So, I should give him a super big hug next time I see him."

"Yes, he definitely deserves it."

I smiled and wrapped my arms around her. "I know

someone else who deserves a hug, too."

"Me? But I almost ruined everything."

"This is for the last fourteen years. If you hadn't been such an amazing coach and friend to me, so many things in my life would've been different. And not for the better."

She hugged me in return with added emotion, and when she stepped back she grasped my hands. "Don't tell anyone I said this, but you've always been my favorite student. I'm not sure what I'm going to do without you around. You've been with me since the first day I started coaching."

Tears pooled in my eyes as our time together flashed before me. We'd experienced every possible high and low, and I wouldn't change any of it. As much as I'd remember the big competitions, what I'd treasure most were the little moments. Things like having a funny fashion show at a shop in Estonia or making up dance moves when hip hop music played at the rink.

"It really is the end of an era, isn't it?"

"If you're trying to make me bawl, you're succeeding," she said, her voice cracking.

We laughed and cried at the same time, and I said, "I'm still going to need you in my new era. Actually, I have a very important position in mind if you say yes."

She gave me a quizzical look, and I wiped the water from my eyes. "We haven't set an exact date yet, but would you be my matron of honor this summer?"

"Oh my gosh, of course I'll say yes!" She hugged me again. "Are you still thinking of doing a beach wedding?"

"That's the plan. As soon as we get home, I have to start getting organized and making calls."

"Anything you need help with, you know I'm here." Her face scrunched with worry. "Do you think Josh's mom will try to butt in on the planning?"

"She might not care about being involved since we'll be out of the limelight once the Olympics are over, but if she does try to make things difficult, I'm not having it. If she'd been any kind of a decent mother to Josh, I'd gladly listen to her opinions, but she dropped that ball a long time ago."

"That is unfortunately the sad truth."

"We're meeting up with her tomorrow night at the P&G Family Home. Josh and I were asked to do a little interview with our families, but he isn't telling her about it. We're shooting at eight, and he told his mom to meet us at nine. He invited Mrs. Cassar to be in the video instead."

"I bet that means a lot to her. She really loves him like a son."

"Josh and I will both be fatherless in the video. My dad's still got that bad cold, so he's going to stay at the hotel and rest up for the Opening Ceremony."

Em scratched her chin. "So, you guys won't be in the Team USA cheer box for the men's and the pairs' shorts tomorrow night."

"We were planning on it, but then this came up. We'll definitely be there Saturday when Liza skates."

"I hope Mrs. Tucker has calmed down about the team event decision?"

A light breeze wisped off the sea, and I edged closer to the railing to feel the sun's warmth. "She's still getting her little comments in, but she's mostly been harping on our engagement and how Josh should've waited to propose here. Specifically, on the ice after our long program so the whole world could see it live, and we could finagle some kind of endorsement out of the publicity."

"She has a one-track mind, doesn't she?"

"Josh said if he'd tattooed dollar signs on his head when he was a kid, she might've paid more attention to him."

Em let out a dry laugh. "That is another sad truth."

I LOOKED AT MY watch and noticed Josh doing the same. We'd been sitting in the main gathering room of the Family Home for almost an hour. The crew filming the video of us had arrived late, and our interviewer, a girl named Pepper with spiked pink hair, was still asking us questions. If they didn't hurry, Mrs. Tucker was going to bust in on us, and we'd be subjected to her unjustified indignation over being excluded.

"I see you ladies visited the complimentary manicure station," Pepper said to Mom and Mrs. Cassar.

"We're all set to cheer on Team USA." Mrs. Cassar flashed her red, white, and blue nails. Her thumbs were painted with stars and stripes.

"Josh, why don't you talk about how Mrs. Cassar has helped you on your Olympic journey."

"Without her, I wouldn't have had an Olympic journey. Besides the incredible financial help she's given me, she's also been a constant source of encouragement and support. I didn't know the true meaning of generosity until I met her." He gave her a warm smile. "She has a heart of gold."

Mrs. Cassar was a tough one to make emotional, but I spied her eyes getting misty. She patted Josh's hand but was speechless. That's when I knew he'd really gotten to her.

"Mrs. Cassar, what's been your favorite part of going on this journey with Josh?" Pepper asked.

She sniffled and cleared her throat. "Watching him grow into the man he's become. He was a great kid when I met him, but he's grown so much since then. I couldn't be more proud to be considered his family."

Josh pulled her in for a hug, and the cameraman zoomed in on their embrace. Mom and I exchanged teary glances, but I froze when Mrs. Tucker entered my sight line. She had eyes on our table and was intently processing the scene.

Oh, hell.

"I think we have everything we need," Pepper said. "It'll be up tomorrow on—"

"What is all this?" Mrs. Tucker asked as she stalked up to the table.

"It was just a quick interview," Josh said.

"Well, if it's about your family then I should be in it." She turned to Pepper. "I'm Josh's mother."

Pepper's mouth hung open, and she looked a little scared. As most people did when they met Mrs. Tucker.

"They still have to talk to a bunch of other athletes." Josh gave Pepper a look that said she'd better not disagree.

"Yes. Sorry. We're on a tight schedule." She picked up her messenger bag. "Thanks again for your time. You can see the video online tomorrow."

She and the cameraman rushed off, and Mrs. Tucker helped herself to the empty chair at our table.

"Did you know you were going to be filmed?" she asked.

Josh hesitated and picked up his bottled water, avoiding her gaze. "No, it just came up."

He was too kind to hurt her feelings by telling her he hadn't wanted her there. If she was even capable of having feelings.

"Roxanne and Evan are about to skate." I pointed to one of the many TVs hanging on the wall, grateful to steer the conversation elsewhere.

"I hope they embarrass themselves so the federation sees what a stupid decision it made," Mrs. Tucker said.

Josh squeezed his bottle, making a loud cracking noise. "Can you please let it go?"

"How can you not be angry that you aren't the ones skating right now?"

"We were angry, but it's done and we're not dwelling on it. We're ecstatic just to be here at all."

Mom and Mrs. Cassar both gasped, and I looked up at the TV. While I'd been watching Josh and his mom argue, Roxanne had splatted on the side-by-side jumps.

Great. Now we're going to hear nothing but "I told you so."

"Let's see how they justify their decision now," Mrs. Tucker said.

"It's just one mistake," I said. I couldn't believe I was defending Roxanne.

No sooner had I spoken than Roxanne hit the ice again, that time on the throw triple flip.

"Now it's two," Mrs. Tucker said with what could only be described as an evil smile.

We watched the rest of the program in awkward silence. When Roxanne and Evan sat in the kiss and cry, their teammates gathered behind them, waving American flags and patriotic pom-poms. Liza patted Evan's shoulder, but she didn't go near Roxanne. I could see in her big blue eyes that she was fuming inside.

Mrs. Tucker excused herself and went over to the refreshments, and she wrangled one of the poor P&G reps into an extended conversation. After that she moved on to anyone else she could find who looked important. When the pairs event ended, Mom and Mrs. Cassar said they needed to start the long trek back to their hotel, so Josh went outside with them to make sure they got into a taxi safely. Mrs. Tucker finally returned to the table, and I shook my head. Once again she'd proven how little she cared about spending time with Josh. It was all about *her*, and I was *so* over it.

"How nice of you to join us," I said sharply.

"Don't pretend like you actually wanted me here tonight."

"You're absolutely right. I didn't want you here and neither did Josh. He lied when he said the video wasn't planned. It's the reason we came here. He didn't want you in it because he wouldn't be able to find anything positive to say about your relationship. How sad is that?"

Her mouth set into a thin line, but I didn't wait for her response. I had so much angry pressure building in my chest that I had to let it out.

"All Josh has wanted his whole life is a mother who loves him for who he is, not for the fame or prestige he can bring to your family. He needed a mother who would play with him as a child, and he needs one now who will genuinely support him. A mother who truly wants what's best for him and wants to see him happy. You've done *none* of that. For twenty-six years you have epically failed. Luckily, Josh has finally found people who do give him all those things. So if you're not going to be the caring and loving mother he deserves, if you're going to continue to always put yourself first, then you should just stay the hell away because he doesn't need any more of your bullshit."

Her lips clamped together even harder, and she glared at me so long I didn't think she would ever speak. When she finally moved, she grabbed her coat from her chair and leaned toward me. Her creamy complexion burned bright red.

"I did not fly halfway around the world to be disrespected and spoken to like this."

She shoved back her chair and blew out the door. As the adrenaline pumping through my veins subsided, I began to tremble. First my hands, then my legs, then everything inside me.

What the hell had I been thinking?

It hadn't been my place to speak for Josh and tell off his mother, no matter how awful she was. I covered my face with my hands and tried to take deep breaths, but I couldn't stop shaking. A hand touched my shoulder, and I jumped.

"What's wrong?" Josh asked.

I peeled my hands away as he sat beside me.

"Did you see your mom leave?" I asked quietly.

His jaw tightened. "What did she say to you?"

"She didn't say anything." I shielded my face again. "I did."

He brushed my hair back and tucked it behind my ear. "Tell me what happened."

"I shouldn't have opened my mouth. I had no business going off like that."

Loud laughter erupted from the next table, and Josh took my hand. "Let's go outside and talk."

I shrugged on my jacket and breathed a little easier when we emerged in the cool, crisp night. We started toward the Village, Josh's arm snugly around my shoulders.

"Whatever you said, I'm sure it was justified," he said.

I kept my focus on the sidewalk, not wanting to look at him. Just thinking of repeating the words put a sour taste in my throat.

"I… I basically told her she was the worst mother ever, you didn't want her here, and she should go away."

His pace slowed, and I stopped us completely. "I'm so sorry. I was so out of line, speaking for you like that. I was just so fed up with her crap. But that doesn't give me the right to tell her those things, especially—"

Josh covered my mouth with his, cutting off my speech and all my thoughts. He softened the kiss, lingering gently on my lips, and then slowly pulled away.

"I had to get you to stop talking," he said.

"I like your method."

"What you said to my mom… it's nothing I haven't thought before and wanted to say myself."

"But I should've let you—"

He placed his finger against my lips. "It's okay. You don't have to apologize."

My shoulders relaxed, and I lightly exhaled. "I was afraid you'd be upset that I put myself in the middle of your relationship. What you want her to know and how you handle it should be up to you."

"Honestly, I'm glad you said something. I've always held onto this little shred of hope that things would somehow change between us, but that's seemed less likely the older and wiser I get. Maybe hearing what you said will make her think, though."

"I don't know if she'll take any of it to heart. She looked more mad than sad, and what I said was damn harsh. I would've been in tears if someone had said those things to me."

"That's because you have a huge heart, and you open it up to other people." He nudged me closer to him. "I've pretty much given up all hope of my mom showing any real emotion."

"She knows how to show hatred. I saw that clearly when we were talking." I shook my head. "And I'd been doing such a good job of keeping my big mouth in check."

"I happen to be very fond of this mouth." He lined my bottom lip with his thumb and followed with a kiss. The warmth he breathed into me erased the last bit of uneasiness I felt.

"I don't want you to spend any more time being upset about this," Josh said. "This is our happy place, and nothing should take away from it."

I smiled and cozied into the curve of his arm. "I love you, Future Husband."

"Back at ya, Future Wife."

We started walking again and took our time strolling through Olympic Park, where all the event venues were conveniently clustered. We passed under the cauldron, where the flame would be ignited at the Opening Ceremony, and I shivered with anticipation. I got the same feeling as we passed the beautiful blue-toned Iceberg Skating Palace, still lit up from the earlier events.

Once inside the Village, we headed for our Team USA building. Josh walked me to my room, and the moment I opened the door, Liza jumped off her bed.

"Did you get the call?" she asked.

"What call?" I checked my phone but had no messages.

"It should be coming any minute now." She grinned and

clasped her hands together, looking like she was about to burst. "You're in. The fed is letting you do the free skate on Saturday."

"What?" Josh and I exclaimed at the same time.

"They're doing this because Roxanne screwed up?" I asked.

"They're doing it because I gave them an ultimatum. Either they give you the free skate or I drop out of mine."

"You blackmailed them?" Josh's eyes doubled in size.

"You're such a boss." I laughed.

"I prefer to think of it as a strategic captain's move. Russia has gold locked up, but we're fighting with Canada and France for silver and bronze. After Roxanne's meltdown tonight, we can't take any chances with them losing points for us again. So, get your game faces on because the team needs you."

"I can't believe—" I put my hands on my head and then hugged Liza, squeezing her with everything in me. "Thank you, thank you, thank you!"

"You rock, Cap." Josh embraced us for a group hug.

"It should've been this way all along. I just righted a wrong."

Josh took a step back. "Our practice in the morning just got really important. We should get to sleep."

He and I shared a joyous goodnight kiss, and I closed the door and turned to a beaming Liza.

"You know what this means?" she said. "The Sochi Pact is *on!*"

I bounced up and down and threw my arms around her again.

CHAPTER THIRTEEN

ALL MY SKATING LIFE I'D LONGED to be surrounded by the Olympic rings, but as I stood backstage at the Iceberg Skating Palace, I was trying my best to avoid looking at them. They were everywhere, and they were just reminding me what a huge moment this was in my career. Josh and I needed to skate well to give the team a boost and keep our chances alive for a spot on the podium.

I brought my eyes up from the concrete floor, and they landed on Em's credential badge, which of course sported the colorful rings. I reached out and flipped it backward, and she gave me a questioning look.

"Don't ask," I said.

Em and Sergei had worried that Josh and I would be tired after the long Opening Ceremony the previous night, but I had so much energy I could do triple run-throughs right now. I was still flying high from walking into the packed stadium in the Parade of Nations and feeling the ultimate confirmation that I belonged there. I'd worn the same patriotic uniform as all the other American athletes, and I'd watched with the same amount of awe as the flame had been lit. I'd finally made it

here, and now I was about to take the next important step —
competing for the first time on Olympic ice.

Our team leader Marni motioned us forward, and Josh
held out his hand to me. I gladly put mine in his and let him
lock our fingers together. We walked toward the ice and
stalled a few yards short of the boards. Josh took my other
hand, and I looked up into his eyes, taking a minute to
reinforce our connection before we had to step onto the ice.

"This is it," I said. "The skate we've always dreamed
about."

The audience applauded the Italian team finishing their
program, and Josh bent his head closer to mine, sealing the
bubble around us. I became totally unaware of the noise and
completely engrossed in the passion in Josh's gaze.

"You and I were meant to be here. In this place. In this
competition. In this moment," he said. "This is our time."

I nodded and stayed lost in his eyes, growing only more
excited to get on the ice and express all my feelings for him
through our skating. He swallowed me in a hug, and I ran my
hands over the strong muscles that lifted me high and held me
up. His love for me did the same, and it had proved to be even
stronger.

Em touched my elbow, so I broke away from Josh and
handed her my jacket. He and I dashed through the ice door,
and cheers rang out from the USA box at the end of the rink. I
sped across the ice and peeked at the Olympic rings painted in
the center. This *was* the biggest moment of my career, and I
had to own it. I hadn't worked my butt off to be afraid of being
in the spotlight. As Josh had said, this was our time, and we
had a kick-ass program to show the world.

I changed direction and skated right over the rings,
spreading my arms wide in the calming technique I'd done for
years. I met up with Josh and joined our hands, and we glided
over to Em and Sergei for their final seconds of coaching.

They both smiled at us, and I felt their strong waves of

pride and positivity. Sergei asked us to put our clasped hands on the boards, and he covered them with his.

"Be one body, breathing together. One heart, beating together. Embrace the power of your love for each other, and you will do amazing things."

Josh and I turned to face one another, and as soon as the announcer introduced us, I shut out everything around us again. We skated to the middle of the rings and claimed our opening spot, standing back to back. I closed my eyes and took deliberate breaths, waiting for the moment I needed to come to life.

As we'd practiced so many times the past nine months, we began our movement on the same piano note and quickly became one with the ice. Our speed made my pulse shoot up as we flew backward into the triple twist. Josh sprang me into the air with snap, and I allowed my muscle memory to take over, spinning three times and landing softly in Josh's solid grip.

We sped past the corner of the rink, and a twinge of fear crept into my stomach. The triple Salchow was next. Before I let myself start doubting my ability again, I internally smacked myself around and thought about how I'd dominated the jump since nationals. *You are all over this. This Salchow answers to YOU.*

We pushed off from the ice, and my mind went blank. My body took charge and powered through three revolutions. With a smooth edge, my right blade hit the ice on the landing, and I saw Josh mirroring me beside me. Perfect jumps. Perfect unison.

Time to let go.

Josh had spent years choreographing the program, and every second had special detail, from the position of our fingers to the slight lean of our bodies toward or away from each other. I was going to make all those details shine. I felt in complete control and more confident than I had ever been on the ice.

Josh assisted me upward once again on the throw triple flip, and I rocketed through the air and rode out the landing on a sweet curve. He skated toward me with the same sureness that I felt, and we conquered our next few elements with so much precision it was as if we'd been skating together our entire lives.

The happiness and love in Josh's eyes made my heart race from more than just adrenaline. Our skates could hardly keep up with the intense vibe between us, and when the music slowed I let out a long breath. Josh pressed me up over his head for our favorite lift, and I let go of his hand so just my stomach rested on his palm. We turned over the ice in circles, and I searched the building for every set of Olympic rings I could find. I wanted to hold onto this memory and this feeling of total bliss forever.

Josh brought my feet back down to earth, but my heart was still in the clouds. We twirled into our combination spin, and I had to refrain from giggling with joy in the midst of changing positions. We were skating at the Olympics, and we'd given the best performance of our lives. None of my daydreams had prepared me for the overpowering feelings I was experiencing. I felt like I had traveled far over the rainbow and was spinning in a magical place beyond my imagination.

We whirled to a stop, and Josh hugged my back to his chest. We stood in almost the exact spot we had begun the program, directly over the rings. I looked down and scratched my toe pick over the green paint, leaving a small mark physically but a large one to me symbolically.

The partisan Russian crowd gave us a bigger ovation than I'd expected. Josh turned me around but kept me in his arms, and he kissed my lips and then my forehead. I held onto his shoulders, so overcome with emotion, and I whispered in his ear, "No words."

When our eyes connected again, our smiles spoke for us.

We acknowledged the audience with heartfelt bows and skated to the ice door, where Em and Sergei were practically leaping over the boards with excitement.

"Wow," Sergei said as he embraced me.

"It was stunning. Absolutely stunning," Em said.

We walked toward the kiss and cry, and Liza met us halfway, tackling us with hugs. "Oh my *God*. That was the best I've ever seen you skate!"

"Guess it's good we saved it for now." I laughed.

Our teammates welcomed us with high-fives and hugs, except Roxanne, who clapped softly while wearing a forced smile. They all stood behind us as we sat on the bench with Em and Sergei, waiting for the score. We wouldn't know until later how the event standings would shake out, but a big number would put pressure on the French and Canadian pairs skating next.

The announcer read the score, and raucous cheers burst out behind us. We'd earned our personal best score ever! Liza choked me with a screeching hug, and Josh and I looped our arms around each other as we led the group backstage. I wanted a minute alone with him, but we got pulled toward the line of media who needed sound bites.

After we answered questions from journalists from around the world, we learned our performance had tightened the standings, and we were in a virtual tie with Canada and France. We changed out of our costumes and finally found some private space near the locker rooms, away from the competition bustle still going strong.

Josh slipped his hands inside the collar of my jacket, and his fingertips tickled the nape of my neck. I pressed up on the toes of my flats and sealed our lips together in a blissful kiss.

"So, this really happened tonight?" I said.

He smiled. "The Daruma didn't let us down."

"I'm so glad I don't have to worry about that thing anymore."

"We did more than reach our goal. We killed it and skated the perfect program."

"Is that how you envisioned it when you drew it up?"

"It was so much better," he said, his thumbs lightly skimming my jaw. "On paper I couldn't feel your incredible energy."

I linked my hands behind his back to draw him closer. "I've never felt that confident in a competitive program before. I wasn't thinking about anything. I was just *feeling*. It was both calming and exhilarating if that makes any sense."

His smile grew wider. "I know exactly what you mean."

"And now tomorrow we might become Olympic medalists. *Olympic medalists.*"

"I'm still trying to process that possibility."

"I've been saying this a lot lately, but I think this moment calls for it more than any other. *What is this life?*"

I CLUTCHED MY MINIATURE American flag in my fist and crossed my legs to stop them from jiggling. Watching my friends compete was more nerve-wracking than getting out there and skating myself. Josh and I sat side by side in the crowded USA box, where we'd just cheered on our teammates in the men's free skate. The next event was the ladies' free skate followed by the free dance. We'd built a small lead over Canada and France and could solidify our position on the podium in the ladies' event, so Liza's performance was going to be pivotal.

Roxanne and Evan came out from backstage, searching our crammed benches for a spot to sit. I scooted over to make room, and Roxanne looked at me like I had a contagious disease. She reluctantly took a seat beside me and stared straight ahead at the ice. She hadn't said a word to me since we'd been in Sochi.

"You know, we all have the same goal here," I said. "We're all on the same team."

She gave me major side eye. "Your ice princess friend better come through."

Oh, no ma'am. You are not going to talk trash about Liza.

"Like you did when you fell on your ass twice?" I said.

Her head whipped in my direction. "You were probably jumping up and down when that happened."

"Actually, I was defending you to my even more annoying future mother-in-law."

"Yeah, she's so annoying to you. I know she's the one who talked the fed into subbing you in."

I couldn't tell her Liza had been our lobbyist or she'd call her something much worse than "ice princess."

"I'm a firm believer in karma," I said. "That's all I'm going to say."

My ex-boyfriend Kyle sat in front of us, and I tapped him on the shoulder and asked if we could switch seats. He shrugged and stood, and I took Josh's hand and brought him down to the lower bench with me. I was already wound up enough without listening to Roxanne make rude comments during Liza's skate.

Sergei stood at the boards with Liza, giving her the encouraging smile I knew so well. She looked gorgeous in her slate blue dress, her raven hair pinned up in a twist. The dress was low on the sparkle factor, which was perfect for the soft and ethereal feel of her program.

The announcer called her name, and I cheered louder than anyone in the building, smacking my hands together and yelling, "Go, Liza!" Josh whistled between his fingers and then leaned forward, his elbows on his thighs. I suspected he felt just as nervous as I did — probably more because he'd choreographed Liza's long program. Having his work displayed by the best skater in the world on the sport's biggest stage was going to take his career to an entirely new level.

The music of Debussy began, and Liza floated across the ice, her posture as strong as that of a ballerina. There was nothing dainty about her athleticism, though. She picked into the ice for her first combination, the triple Lutz-triple toe loop, and she sprang into the air as high as some of the guys did on their jumps. Her landings couldn't be smoother, and I whooped and rubbed my sweaty palms on my jeans.

Josh stared intensely at the ice, and his head bobbed up and down as if he was doing the steps along with Liza. I hooked my arm through his and tried to relax with the beautiful music, but my jumpy knees wouldn't stay still. Liza skated toward our end of the rink, and she pushed off from the ice for the triple loop. I sucked in a breath as soon as she went up. Her body was tilted *way* off axis. She came down with the same lean and tumbled to the ice.

Roxanne cursed quietly behind me, and I held on tighter to Josh, both to keep me from slapping her and to steady my now heart-attack-level pulse. Liza settled right back into the choreography, and she proved her champion status by doing a textbook double Axel.

The rest of her jumps came just as easily, and I leapt from the bench the second she spun to a stop at center ice. We all piled out of the box, cheering our way over to the kiss and cry to wait for her. After she donned her skate guards and got a big hug from Sergei, I ran up to her and flung my arms around her as she had done to me.

"You were so awesome."

"The stupid loop," she mumbled.

"You dominated everything else. You did your job and then some."

We stepped into the kiss and cry, and Josh and I positioned ourselves right behind her as the judges finished punching in their scores. Liza needed to finish first to give us enough points for the team silver medal. I remembered the previous competitor's score and attempted to do the necessary math in my head, but I couldn't focus. I was on sensory overload with the buzz of the crowd and the bright lights and the jitters that had returned. It was taking an awfully long time for the score.

The announcer's voice quieted the noise, and I watched the video board closely. She read the numbers, and I grabbed Josh's hand as she paused before giving us the placement. *Come on, come on…*

"She is in first place," the announcer boomed. "Team USA is currently in second place."

Screams and shouts of glee exploded from all of us. Amidst the chaos of hugs and high-fives I even hugged Roxanne. Josh and I embraced and looked at each other with disbelief, both of us sputtering things like "This is crazy!" and "I can't believe this!" We had a big enough lead over Team Canada that they wouldn't be able to surpass us in the ice dance event. We were the silver medalists. *Olympic silver medalists.*

Liza was smiling but not nearly as exuberantly as the others, and I knew she was still mad at herself for the missed jump. I put my arm across her shoulders and walked with her ahead of everyone as we headed backstage.

"This was your practice run. You're going to be even more amazing for your individual event."

"That's almost word for word what my dad said. I think you've been his student for too long." She elbowed my side.

She had to join the media circus so we split up, and I noticed Josh looking serious as he stared at his phone.

"What's up?" I asked.

"My mom texted me, asking to meet her upstairs."

We hadn't heard from Mrs. Tucker since she'd stormed out of the Family House. Not even after we'd skated. I wasn't sure if she'd taken my advice to the extreme and had hopped on a plane back to California.

"I'm going to apologize to her," I said.

"You don't have to. What you said was true."

"I know, but I could've said it a better way."

He shot her back a quick reply, and we left the restricted area and entered the concourse of the arena. Spectators crowded the concession stands, trying to grab snacks before the free dance started. We found Mrs. Tucker away from the mob, standing near one of the exits. I steeled myself for God knew what she was going to say to me.

"Hey," Josh said.

"I was going to text you last night, but I knew you would be busy with media. Frankly, I was expecting to hear from one or both of you first." She glared at me. "With an apology."

"I am sorry about the other night," I said. "I should've tried to have a conversation with you instead of attacking you."

"You shouldn't have said anything at all," she snapped.

"Yes, she should have," Josh said. "I agree with all of it."

Mrs. Tucker lifted her chin, and her eyes bore the same angry look she'd had with me. "You're saying you don't want me here? You don't want me in your life?"

"If you're not here for the right reasons, then no. I don't."

"What do you consider the right reasons?"

Josh pinched the bridge of his nose. "If you have to ask, then this discussion is pointless."

"I am your mother. What other reason do I need to be here?"

I clamped my lips together, itching to enlighten her. But I had to let Josh handle this.

"It has to be about more than a title," he said. "There has to be some meaningful substance behind it."

Mrs. Tucker folded her arms and shook her head. "After everything I gave you, all the opportunities—"

"When I said substance, I didn't mean material things. You don't—" Josh let out a frustrated breath. "You just don't understand, and I don't know that you ever will."

My phone vibrated in my jacket pocket, and I debated whether I should check it. If the text was from someone in the federation, it could be important.

I pulled it from my jacket and heard a quiet huff from Mrs. Tucker. I quickly read the text and hid the phone again.

"Marni said they need us downstairs," I said to Josh.

"We can continue this later," Mrs. Tucker said.

Josh looked at her for a long minute, resignation settling in his eyes, and he took a small step backward. "There's nothing to continue. I've said everything I needed to."

"So that's it. You're just dismissing me."

"It's up to you where we go from here."

He palmed the small of my back, and I followed his lead. We fought the crowd to get to the security checkpoint, and once we were backstage, I held him up before we met up with our teammates.

"You okay?"

He nodded and raked his hand through his hair. "I feel kinda relieved. I'm glad it's all out there."

"It really is up to her whether you can ever have a real relationship."

"I don't see the point in going on like we have been. It's so meaningless. Steph has started distancing herself from her, too. She just doesn't want to deal with it anymore, and I feel the same way."

"I'm glad you and Steph have gotten closer these past few years."

"Me too." He cupped my shoulders and stared into my eyes. "And she's not the only family I have. I've got you and Mrs. Cassar and your parents and even Em and Sergei. I couldn't ask for more."

I smiled and wrapped him in my arms. I couldn't ask for more either.

TWENTY-FOUR HOURS LATER, I still had a hard time believing I was an Olympic medalist. The Sochi organizers had bucked tradition and weren't giving out medals at the ice arena, so we'd had to wait a full day to receive our hardware at the nightly ceremony in Olympic Park. Twenty thousand people packed the Medals Plaza, and I stood with my eight teammates just offstage, waiting for the regal music to begin. We all looked super sharp in our silver puffy jackets with the Team USA logo.

"This has been the longest day in the history of days," I joked.

"You're dying to get your hands on that bling," Josh said.

"What can I say? I love pretty, shiny things."

We got the cue to line up for our entrance, so we situated ourselves with Liza at the front of our group. The music began, and chills shot through me. I bounced on the heels of my sneakers, and behind me Josh squeezed my waist. I turned and flashed him a huge grin.

We walked out onto the stage, and the sea of people went bananas, mostly because Team Russia was marching out as the champions. Canada followed them as the bronze medalists, and all of us stopped behind our respective steps on the podium.

Canada received their medals first, and then the attention shifted to us. The eight of us clasped hands and looked at each other, and we all stepped up onto the podium at the same time, raising our arms in celebration. My chills multiplied as the crowd gave us lots of love. I spied a number of American flags and signs of support in the throng.

The presenters went down the line, bestowing the medals, and my throat constricted as my name was announced. I bent forward and accepted the ribbon around my neck, marveling at how heavy the medal was. While Josh received his, I placed the large silver disc in my palm and lifted it to my lips. Josh did the same, and we couldn't stop smiling at each other.

"This is insane." He shook his head.

"I'm never taking this off," I said. "I'm just gonna wear it like jewelry."

Liza leaned forward and caught my eye, and she gave me a double thumbs-up. I tapped my heart and pointed to her, hoping she knew how incredibly grateful I was that she'd made this happen for us.

After Russia was adorned with their gold medals, everyone silenced for the raising of the flags and the Russian national anthem. I watched the Stars and Stripes ascend into the dark night, the Olympic flame burning brightly behind it, and I trembled with excitement and happiness and pride. Tears collected in my eyes and dripped down my cheeks. This was another moment I wanted to burn into my memory and relive over and over the rest of my life.

I looked down at my glossy medal and then up at Josh's gorgeous profile, and my tears of joy flowed stronger. I had my dream bling around my neck and on my finger and more love in my heart than I'd ever thought possible.

EPILOGUE

"DOES THIS LOOK STRAIGHT?" I ASKED Josh as I stepped back from the wall. Inside the display box were our silver medals plus photos of the two of us on the ice and our team on the podium. It was the first thing I'd hung in the living room of our new apartment.

Josh looked up from plugging in his keyboard, and he squinted with one eye closed. "Looks perfect."

I stared at the photos and recalled all the wonderful days we'd spent in Sochi. Josh and I had finished fifth in the pairs event with two more spectacular performances, and we'd made so many new friends from different sports around the world. I couldn't have written a better ending to our competitive career.

Spinning around, I looked for the next box I should unpack. We'd emptied most of them, and the cozy apartment already felt like home. It was a short commute from Boston College, so I would be set in the fall, and it was also an easy T ride from the studio space Josh had rented.

I rolled up my T-shirt sleeves and reached into my box labeled "Fun Stuff," pulling out a stack of CDs. As I shelved them in the entertainment center, I smiled at one in particular.

"We should play this at the wedding." I laughed and showed Josh the *Mickey Unrapped* CD.

"We should. That was the first gift I ever gave you."

Even though over four years had passed since that night, I could still vividly remember the yearning look in Josh's eyes and how our kisses had come as hard and fast as the rain against the car.

I hummed softly and filed the disc onto the shelf. "That was such a hot night."

Josh broke into a slow grin. "I miss our car make-out sessions."

"I'm game anytime you are."

He was about to say something, but his laptop rang on the bistro table between the living room and the kitchen. He clicked to answer the video call, and Stephanie's face popped up on the screen.

"What's up?" Josh said.

"I'm melting. Why is New York so hot?"

"Welcome to summer in the northeast."

I sat next to Josh in front of the webcam and enlarged the video. "How's the new job going?"

"It's insane. This is the first day I've been home before ten."

"Have you had time to work on the dress alterations?" I asked as I chewed my thumbnail. The wedding was only a few weeks away.

"I almost fell asleep on my sewing machine last night, but yes. And I added a little something I think you're going to like. I personally think it's fabulous." She reached off camera. "Josh, go away. You can't see this."

He laughed and pushed his chair back. "I know. Court has already warned me about peeking at photos on her phone."

He got up and went into the kitchen, and I leaned closer

to the computer. Stephanie held up my dress, and I gasped.

"How much do you love it?" she said.

The off-white dress had a simple halter neckline that cut into a deep V, and the skirt flowed softly down to my toes. None of that had changed. The addition was a narrow, pale pink sash tied around the waist with tiny flowers accenting the back.

"Oh my God, it's perfect!"

Josh took a few steps toward the table. "How can I watch you have that reaction and not die of curiosity?"

"Don't you dare come any closer." I held up my hand like a stop sign.

Stephanie hid the dress off screen. "It's safe now. You can look."

"We should drive down next weekend to pick it up." Josh returned to his seat. "We can see your new place."

"I'll probably be working the whole time, but you're welcome to my couch."

"You're not going to have trouble getting time off for the wedding, are you?" I asked.

"I told my boss the first day that this vacation time is non-negotiable."

Josh smiled. "I had no doubt you'd lay down the law."

Stephanie swept her long hair over one shoulder and combed her fingers through it. "What did you decide to do about Mom and Dad?"

"We're not inviting them. They barely talked to us at your graduation, and they didn't even ask about the wedding."

"I doubt they'd show even if they were invited," she said.

Josh shrugged. "I don't let it bother me anymore. As long as you're there, that's all that matters to me."

Stephanie dipped her head, but she couldn't hide her smile. She cleared her throat and said, "Well, I have no problem representing the family."

Her phone trilled, and she made a face as she picked it

up. "Ugh, it's work. I have to get it."

"Go ahead. We'll talk later about next weekend," Josh said.

"Thank you again for all your work on the dress!" I said as I waved goodbye.

The video call disconnected, and Josh went back to setting up his keyboard. I finished unpacking the CDs and then drifted over to him, watching him carefully clean the keys.

"Are you ready to christen the apartment with a song?" I asked.

He smiled and slid onto the small bench. "I know exactly the one to play."

I stood behind him with my hands resting lightly on his shoulders, and he set his fingers on the keys. I had an idea what he might play, and my heart warmed at the first few notes. My favorite rendition of "Over the Rainbow." I angled forward and kissed his cheek, and I watched as his hands filled our new home with beautiful noise.

As he pressed the final key he turned to smile at me, and I wound my arms around him. He pulled me onto his lap, and our lips came together in a long, slow kiss that also hit all the right notes.

"This is officially our place now," he said between sweet kisses on my lips and my neck and my shoulder.

"I love the sound of that." I threaded my fingers into his hair. "Our place."

"It's still blowing my mind that we're going to be a married couple in a few weeks."

"Let's make a vow that we'll never be an old, boring married couple. Even when we're shuttling kids to ballet practice and baseball games and attending PTA meetings."

"Us? Boring? Not possible. We're going to be the cool couple all the other parents aspire to be. They'll want all our secrets."

"And what will our secrets be?"

He thought a minute. "Number one — any time we feel stressed we have a lip sync party."

I laughed. "I like that."

"Number two." He slipped the rubber band from my ponytail and gently untangled my curls. "I make my wife feel appreciated and desired every single day."

"I really, *really* like that."

"Number three — we always find time to talk to each other, no matter how crazy our schedules are."

I smiled and tipped our foreheads together, and he said, "We also find time to play, no matter how busy we are."

"Is that the code word we'll use around our kids? 'Mommy and Daddy need play time tonight?'"

"Yes." He grinned. "Totally."

"Can I add one?"

"Of course."

"I tell my husband every single day how much I love him." I laid my hand on his chest. "And how much I want him."

I trailed my fingers down to his stomach, tracing the hard ridges under his soft T-shirt. He buried his hands deeper in my hair and guided my mouth toward his. His lips seared mine, sparking heat in the far corners of my body, and I melted into him. No way could we ever be boring. Not when Josh made me feel *this* every time he touched me.

"How do you do it?" I murmured against his lips.

"How do I do what?"

"Give me *all* the feelings."

I felt his smile as his mouth brushed mine. "That's one secret I can't reveal."

"Hmm… are you sure?" I kissed his throat, lingering over his quickening pulse.

"Playing dirty, I see."

He tickled my sides, and I squirmed and succumbed to

giggles. Swallowing my laughter with a kiss, he stilled me in his arms, and I basked again in the love he gave me. A lifetime of all the feelings awaited us, and I couldn't wait to get started.

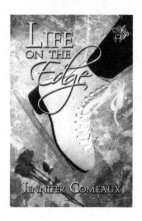

PREVIEW

Before the Ice Series came the Edge Series. Discover how
Emily and Sergei's love story began in this excerpt from
Life on the Edge.

June, 2000
    BAM!

MY ELBOW WHACKED CHRIS'S forehead for the fourth time
during practice. He grunted and caught me before I hit the ice.
Though I'd skated over half of my nineteen years, I'd never
had so many collisions. Of course, until a year ago, I'd never
skated with a partner.

I cringed and touched Chris's sweaty brow. "I'm so
sorry."

"It's okay." He raked his hand through his thick dark
hair. "A little head trauma never hurt anyone."

I laughed wearily and arched my neck, stretching the sore
muscles. The cold air wasn't helping to loosen them. Looking
up, my eyes honed in on the red, white, and blue banner

above the rink:

Emily Butler and Christopher Grayden—2000 National Silver Medalists

Only four months had passed since Chris and I placed second at our first national championship, but it seemed like a lifetime. The triple twist, the high-flying element we needed to learn before next season, continued to elude me. *If we don't master this move, we'll never compete with the top teams in the world.*

I grasped Chris's hand. "Let's try it again."

We took matching determined strokes across the ice, and the burst of wind cooled my face and loosened damp tendrils from my long ponytail. With a quick motion, Chris squeezed my hips and launched me into the air. I wound myself tight and spun but fell into Chris's waiting arms before finishing three revolutions. A sigh heaved my shoulders.

Sergei glided toward us around the other practicing skaters. Our coach was often mistaken for one of us because of his youth. He nodded and regarded us with his deep blue eyes. "The rotation is getting faster. Focus on what you did right today. I see a lot of improvement."

I relaxed into a smile. Before I'd started working with Sergei, I'd heard many horror stories about Russian coaches. Sergei demanded discipline and maximum effort, but his energy stayed positive, and he provided constant encouragement.

Chris and I left the ice and sat on the short set of wooden bleachers. My ankles thanked me as I untied my skate laces and gave them space to breathe.

"I guess it's an improvement I didn't give you another black eye," I said.

Chris poked his swollen freckled cheek. "I kinda like my shiner. Makes me look tough." He grinned, displaying his dimples.

"You're going to need more than that to make you look

tough," I teased as I walked away.

Inside the locker room, the musty scent of sweat and metal contrasted with the cool freshness of the ice. After stowing my skates in my locker and slipping on a pair of sneakers, I pulled a fitted T-shirt over my leotard and winced as I bumped the fresh bruises on my arms. If people only knew how much pain went into chasing the Olympic dream...

I needed to talk to Sergei before his next lesson, and I found him in the rink's upstairs lounge, which overlooked the ice. He was holding a cup of coffee and talking to a couple of the skating moms. As usual, they sat captivated, totally engrossed in his words, and I couldn't blame them. When I'd met Sergei, I stammered through our introduction, spellbound by his captivating eyes and gleaming smile. His personable manner had quickly put me at ease, though, and I'd gotten past staring at his good looks. Important, obviously, if I wanted to get any work done on the ice.

As Sergei spoke to the moms, I remembered I had to phone my own mother. She expected a daily call once I'd moved from Boston to Cape Cod a year ago. I lingered near the water cooler and read the announcements stapled to the bulletin board until Sergei finished his conversation and moved toward the stairs.

"Sergei, do you have a minute?"

"Sure." He glanced at his sport watch. "I have about ten. What's up?"

"I was thinking of doing some coaching in the afternoons like I used to do in Boston. Just a few kids, but I wanted to see what you thought." I toyed with my silver cross and chain. "If it might be too much to take on right now."

He took a long sip of coffee and gave me a pensive look. "I might have a better idea. Walk with me."

I followed him down the narrow steps to the rink, and he set his paper cup on the boards. Skaters swooshed past us, creating a chilly breeze.

"Would you be interested in helping me with one of my novice teams?" Sergei asked. "Teaching them the pair elements would reinforce everything you've learned."

I bobbed my head with vigor at his show of confidence. "That sounds like a great idea."

He spread his hands apart. "Don't I always have all the answers?"

"Yes, Oh Great and All-Knowing Coach." I performed a playful bow.

"I've never had an assistant before. Maybe you should call me 'Mister Petrov' when we work together." He lifted his cup to his mouth, a hint of a smile on his lips.

"You're joking, right?"

His eyes widened with innocence. "Why would I be joking?"

"You're only six years older than me." I laughed and started for the weight room, and Sergei chuckled behind me. "I'm not calling you 'Mister.'"

WITHIN A WEEK, I began assisting Sergei with his newest and youngest team of twelve-year-old Courtney and fourteen-year-old Mark. They were struggling with their double loop throw jump, so I acted as Sergei's partner to demonstrate the technique. The kids stood next to the boards while Sergei's strong hands grasped my hips and vaulted me across the ice. A double felt light and easy compared to the triples I normally did.

Courtney and Mark studied us attentively and tried the throw on their own. Attempt after attempt, Courtney failed to land on a clean edge. Her pink cheeks deepened to crimson as she huffed with frustration.

"It's alright." Sergei patted her shoulder. "Mark, she needs a little more height. Make sure you've got your weight balanced on the takeoff."

"Courtney, also try pulling in tighter and quicker." I brought my arms sharply against my chest.

Our students worked on the element each afternoon, some days having more success than others, but Sergei never lost patience. Watching him handle Courtney and Mark's roller coaster of emotions with gentle authority gave me a new level of respect for him. He knew just how to reassure the kids and light up their eyes with understanding.

After Courtney and Mark's sessions, I often stopped at the Starbucks near the rink on my way home. I learned Sergei was a frequent patron, too, and every time we ran into each other, our conversations grew longer.

One afternoon, we finally gravitated to one of the tiny tables and had been sitting there over half an hour. Sergei had gone to the counter for a refill, and when he rejoined me, he caught me softly singing Sting's "Fields of Gold" along with the piped-in radio.

"Are you a Sting fan?" he asked, stirring a packet of sugar into his black coffee.

"Huge." I sipped my latte. "Are you?"

"I have all his CDs. 'Fields of Gold' is one of my favorite songs."

I leaned forward and rested my elbows on the small table. "Did you know he's having a concert up in Mansfield next weekend? None of my friends want to go. They said his music is for old people." I frowned.

Sergei laughed. "Yeah, I don't know anyone interested in going either."

"I wonder if there are tickets left. Maybe we could go together."

He stared at me over his cup, and I shifted backward in my seat. I hoped he didn't think I was suggesting anything like a date. The U.S. Figure Skating Federation wouldn't approve of a coach and student dating.

I hastily added, "You know, since no one else wants to go… and we don't know when he'll have another show here."

Sergei nodded and his mouth gradually opened into a smile. "Yeah, we should go. The last concert I went to was about five years ago, right after I moved to Chicago from Moscow. It was Dave Matthews Band. I hadn't heard of them, but some people at the rink invited me."

"Ahh, I love them. I've never seen them live."

"They were great. Turned me into a big fan." He tapped his fingers on his cup. "But what I remember most about that night was the taxi ride home. I didn't have a car, and I lived *way* outside the city. The taxi driver didn't speak good English and neither did I at the time. I fell asleep, and when he woke me up, I had no idea where we were. He'd misunderstood me and taken me to a town twenty miles from where I lived."

I burst into laughter. "Oh, no!"

"When he finally got me home, I didn't have enough cash to pay the ridiculous fare, and we got in an argument about whose fault it was he took me to the wrong place." He chuckled and shook his head. "I gave him all the money I had and left him outside my apartment, cursing me out."

Giggles echoed in my throat. "That's crazy. Well, the good news is we can drive ourselves to Mansfield. Speaking of which, I should get home and check on the tickets." I snagged my car keys from my purse. "If I find some, I'll go ahead and order them."

"Let me know later how much I owe you."

"Don't worry, I won't curse you out if you don't pay me right away." I smiled, and Sergei laughed.

With my keys in one hand and my coffee in the other, I stood and aimed for the door. "I'll call you when I get them!"

Typical summertime traffic slowed my drive home. I loved the beauty of the Cape during summer with the hydrangeas in bloom and the deep orange sunsets, but I missed the peacefulness of winter on the island. After crawling bumper to bumper on Route Six from South Dennis to Hyannis, I finally arrived at my parents' vacation townhouse, which had become my year-round home.

In the sun-splashed living room, my roommate Aubrey was hunched over one of her ice dance costumes, needle and thread in hand.

"What happened to your dress?" I dropped down beside her on the beige chenille couch.

She pushed a few stray blond hairs out of her eyes and squinted at the pink fabric. "Some stones fell off last time I wore it."

I picked up my laptop from the coffee table and drummed my fingers while it booted up. With a few clicks, I landed on Ticketmaster.com.

Aubrey glanced at the screen. "What are you buying tickets for?"

"Sting's concert in Mansfield. Turns out Sergei is as big a fan as I am."

Her perfectly-shaped eyebrows curved upward. "You're going on a road trip with Sergei?"

"Mansfield is an hour away. I don't call that a road trip."

She straightened the short skirt of the costume and examined the shimmering silver stones around the hem. "You two seem pretty chummy these days," she said with a sidelong glance.

I shrugged. "We like to talk when we get coffee. No big deal."

"It's a big deal when you start going out at night together. Coaches aren't supposed to be that friendly with their students. Especially not young, hot coaches."

My face warmed, and I focused on the computer screen. "We work together and have a few common interests. It's nothing more."

"I'm just trying to look out for you, Em. You need to be careful."

My fingers paused on the keyboard. Aubrey was the same age as me, but her dating history could fill a book three times the size of mine. She'd been breaking hearts since I'd met her at thirteen. Our gap in boyfriend experience sometimes led her to treat me like a little sister.

"Sergei and I have a professional relationship. You don't need to worry."

She didn't look convinced, but she didn't press the issue. I turned back to the computer and concentrated on selecting two seats for the concert, ignoring the tiny voice in my head that echoed Aubrey's warning.

A RUMBLE OF THUNDER rolled in the distance, and both Sergei and I looked skyward. Fast moving clouds hid the moon. A roof covered half the amphitheater but not our seats in the farthest reaches of the venue. Sting had finished his first set, and I was regretting not bringing my rain slicker.

Sergei rose from the long bench. "Do you want a soda or anything?"

"I'll take a bottle of water." I reached into my jeans pocket for the cash I'd stashed.

He waved away the money. "I've got it."

I smiled as I watched his long legs take him down the packed aisle. I hadn't been on a date in so long that I'd forgotten how nice it was having a guy do the little things like fight the crowd for concessions and... *Wait a second.* I shook my head. *This isn't a date, remember?* Just because Sergei opened his car door for me and wiped the dirt off my seat at the amphitheater didn't mean our outing was anything more than friendly. *He was being polite.*

The smell of popcorn wafted past me as people returned from the concession stand and climbed into our row. Sergei came back with two bottles of water and handed me one.

"This is definitely the best concert I've been to," he said.

"I saw U2 a few years ago in Boston, and they blew me away." I paused, and Sergei raised an eyebrow. "But so far, this is even better."

A lone raindrop plopped on my nose, and my eyes drifted to the sky again. "I think we're about to get drenched."

A few more drops fell, and Sergei said, "If it gets too bad, we can leave if you want."

"No way. I don't wanna miss any of the show. Unless you're afraid you're going to melt?" I bit my bottom lip to stifle a smile.

He laughed. "No, I can handle it."

The drops soon increased to a steady drizzle and pelted us on and off through the rest of the show. I sang along to every song while the rain coated my lips. Next to me, Sergei patted his leg in time to the beat of each tune, and every now and then, his arm bumped mine. His skin felt warm despite being wet, and with each touch my arm tingled.

By the time Sting finished his second encore, my navy T-shirt clung to me and my hair was soaked, but I was too awed by the music to care. I peeked at Sergei, and his short golden brown hair had darkened from the rain, making his blue eyes stand out even more. We moved with the thick crowd to the parking lot and had just hopped into Sergei's SUV when the drizzle became a downpour.

"We got out of there right in time," I said.

"You mean you wouldn't want to sit outside in this? What, afraid you would melt, Emily?"

I laughed. "Oh, I could've handled it."

The windshield wipers slapped back and forth, drowning out the classic rock on the radio. Sergei turned on the heater and drove slowly until we reached the interstate and pointed south to the Cape.

"I'm so glad we came," he said. "He sounded amazing live."

I combed my fingers through my hair, unknotting the long, damp waves. "I know. I'd see him again in a heartbeat."

"Next time he comes, we'll have to get tickets early so we can be closer to the stage." He shot me a smile. "And out of the rain."

"Definitely." I returned his smile.

A shiver sped down my spine at the thought of spending another evening with Sergei. I didn't know if I was still on a high from the concert, but being in the dark car with him was heightening all my senses. I'd always thought he was attractive, but only now did I notice how his smile softened the sharp angles of his face, how sexy my name sounded in his Russian accent, how his T-shirt hugged his lean yet muscular chest.

I gulped and set my eyes on the highway in front of us. *You need to put those thoughts out of your mind right now.*

BOOKS BY JENNIFER COMEAUX

To stay up to date on Jennifer's new releases, join her mailing list:
http://eepurl.com/UZjMP

Ice Series
Crossing the Ice (Ice #1)
Losing the Ice (Ice #2)

Edge Series
Life on the Edge (Edge #1)
Edge of the Past (Edge #2)
Fighting for the Edge (Edge #3)

Jennifer loves to hear from readers! Visit her online at:
jennifercomeaux.blogspot.com
www.twitter.com/LadyWave4
jcomeaux4@gmail.com

Please consider taking a moment to leave a review at the applicable retailer. It is much appreciated!

ACKNOWLEDGEMENTS

My first thank you must always go to my faithful beta readers — Teresa, Christy, Sylvianne, and Debbie. And thank you, Christy and Melissa, for proofreading!

I have to thank two of my favorite pair skaters, Marissa Castelli and Tarah Kayne, for answering my research questions. You are both such fierce competitors and have given me so much inspiration when writing my pair girls!

Two more favorite skaters, Alex Shaughnessy and Jimmy Morgan, also deserve thanks for once again taking time out of their training day to pose for my cover. You make gorgeous models! And a big shout-out to Marni Gallagher for volunteering to take the photos and doing such an amazing job.

My final thank you goes out to all the readers. You keep me going when I hit mental blocks, and your excitement over my characters and their stories never ceases to put a huge smile on my face. Thank you for giving my books a chance!

ABOUT THE AUTHOR

JENNIFER COMEAUX is a tax accountant by day, writer by night. There aren't any ice rinks near her home in south Louisiana, but she's a diehard figure skating fan and loves to write stories of romance set in the world of competitive skating. One of her favorite pastimes is travelling to competitions, where she can experience all the glitz and drama that inspire her writing.